THE
STORMY
PETREL

THE
STORMY
PETREL

Mary Stewart

DOUBLEDAY DIRECT LARGE PRINT EDITION

FAWCETT CREST • NEW YORK

This Large Print Edition, prepared especially for Doubleday Direct, Inc., contains the complete unabridged text of the original Publisher's Edition.

A Fawcett Crest Book
Published by Ballentine Books
Copyright © 1991 by Mary Stewart

Line drawings by Gavin Rowe

All rights reserved under International and Pan-American Copyright Conventions. Published in the United States by Ballentine Books, a division of Random House, Inc., New York.

No part of this book may be reproduced or utilized in any form or by any means, electronic or mechanical, including photocopying, recording, or by any information storage or retrieval system, without permission in writing from the Publisher. Inquiries should be addressed to Permissions Department, William Morrow and Company, Inc., 1350 Avenue of the Americas, New York, N.Y. 10019.

ISBN 0-7394-0796-1

This edition published by arrangement with William Morrow and Company, Inc.

Manufactured in the United States of America

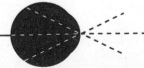

**This Large Print Book carries the
Seal of Approval of N.A.V.H.**

Dedicated to
Culcicoides Pulicaris Argyllensis
with respect

CHAPTER 1

I must begin with a coincidence which I would not dare to recount if this were a work of fiction. Coincidences happen daily in "real life" which would be condemned in a mere story, so writers tend to avoid them. But they happen. Daily, they happen. And on this particular day they—or rather it— happened twice.

I was working in my room, when a knock at the door heralded the entry of four second-year students. Usually I welcome them. They are my job. As English tutor at Haworth College in Cambridge I deal with them every day. But on this sunny afternoon in May, as it happened, I would not have welcomed any intruder, even the college servant with a Recorded Delivery letter announcing a big win in a government lottery. I was writing a poem.

They say that after the age of thirty, or

marriage, whichever comes first, one can write no more poetry. It is true that after the age of thirty certain poets seem to be incapable of writing much that is worth reading; there are notable exceptions, but they only serve to prove the rule. Actually, I believe that the marriage rule applies only to women, which says something for what marriage is supposed to do for them, but on that sunny Tuesday afternoon neither of the disqualifying conditions applied to me. I was twenty-seven, unmarried, heart-whole for the time being, and totally immersed in my work.

Which is why I should have welcomed the students who wanted to talk to me about the poetry of George Darley, which a misguided colleague of mine had included in a series of lectures on the early nineteenth century, and in so doing had worried the more discerning of my students, who were failing to see any merit there. But I had been visited that morning by what was usually at this stage of the term a rare inspiration, and was writing a poem of my own. More important than George Darley? At any rate better, which would not be difficult. As a struggling poet in the late twentieth century, I often thought that some early poets achieved publication very easily. But I did not say so to my students. Let them now praise famous men. They do it so rarely that it is good for them.

I said "Come in," sat them down, listened and then talked and finally got rid of them and went back to my poem. It had gone. The first stanza lay there on my desk, but the idea, the vision had fled like the dream dispelled by Coleridge's ill-starred person from Porlock. I reread what I had written, wrestled with the fading vision for a few sweating minutes, then gave up, swore, crumpled the page up, pitched it into the empty fireplace, and said, aloud:

"What I really need is a good old-fashioned ivory tower."

I pushed my chair back, then crossed to the open window and looked out. The lime trees were glorious in their young green, and, in default of the immemorial elms, the doves were moaning away in them like mad. Birds were singing their heads off everywhere, and from the clematis beside the window came the scent of honey and the murmur of innumerable bees. Tennyson; now there, I thought, was one of the really honourable exceptions to the rule, never

failing, never fading even in old age, while
I, at twenty-seven, could not even finish a
lyric that had seemed, only a short while
ago, to be moving inevitably towards the final tonic chord.

Well, so I was not Tennyson. I was probably, come to that, not even George Darley.
I laughed at myself, felt better, and settled
down on the window-seat in the sun to enjoy what was left of the afternoon. *The
Times,* half read and then abandoned, lay
on the seat beside me. As I picked it up to
throw it aside, a line of small print caught
my eye.

"Ivory tower for long or short let. Isolated
cottage on small Hebridean island off the
coast of Mull. Ideal for writer or artist in
search of peace. Most relatively mod. cons."
And a box number.

I said, aloud: "I don't believe it."

"What don't you believe, Dr. Fenemore?"

One of my students had come back, and
was hesitating in the open doorway. It was
Megan Lloyd, who was the daughter of a
Welsh farm worker from somewhere in
Dyfed, and who had earned her place in
College with a brilliant scholarship. Short,
rather thickset, with dark curling hair, dark

eyes, and freckles, she looked as if she would be most at home with dogs and horses, or with bared arms scrubbing a dairy down, and perhaps she was, but she was also very intelligent, highly imaginative, and easily my best student. Some day, with average luck, she would be a good writer. I remembered that I had promised to see her about some poems she had written and had nervously asked me to read. She looked nervous still, but half amused with it, as she added:

"Surely, *The Times*? It's not supposed to get things wrong, is it?"

"Oh, Megan, come in. Sorry, was I talking to myself? It's nothing, I was off on a track of my own for a moment. Yes, I've got your file here, and yes, I've read them." I went back to my desk, picked the folder up, and gestured her to a chair. She looked back at me with no expression at all in her face, but her eyes were twice as big as usual, and I could see the tension in every muscle. I know how she felt. Every time your work is read, you die several deaths for every word, and poetry is like being flayed alive.

So I went straight to it. "I liked them. Some of them very much. And of course some not so much . . ." I talked on about the poems, while she slowly relaxed and began to look happy, and even, in the end, cheerfully argumentative, which, with Megan, was par for the course. At length I closed the folder.

"Well, there you are, as far as I'm able to judge. Whether some of the more, shall I say, advanced judgments of the day will concur is something I can't guess at, but if you want to try and publish, go ahead and good luck to you. Whatever happens, you must go on writing. Is that what you wanted to hear?"

She swallowed, cleared her throat, then nodded without speaking.

I handed her the folder. "I won't say anything more here and now. I've written fairly detailed notes about some of them. I think it would be better—and we would both find it easier—if you looked at those in your own time? And of course if there's anything you don't understand, or want to argue about, please feel free. All right?"

"Yes. Thank you. Thank you very much for all the trouble. It was just that I—that one doesn't know oneself—"

"Yes, I know."

She smiled, her face lighted suddenly

from within. "Of course you do. And in return, am I allowed to give *you* some advice?"

"Such as what?" I asked, surprised.

She glanced down at the empty hearth, where the crumpled page had fallen and partly unfurled. It would be obvious even from where she sat that the sheet contained lines of an unfinished poem, disfigured with scoring and the scribbles of frustration.

She repeated, with a fair imitation of my voice, but with a smile that robbed the echo of any sting of impertinence: " 'Whatever happens, you must go on writing.' " Then suddenly, earnestly: "I can't read it from here, but I'm sure you shouldn't throw it away. Give it another go, won't you, Dr. Fenemore? I loved that last one of yours in the *Journal*. Please."

After a pause that seemed endless, I said, rather awkwardly: "Well, thank you. But in term time . . . One can't choose one's times, you see."

"Can one ever?"

"I suppose not."

"I'm sorry, I shouldn't have said that." Suddenly embarrassed, she gathered her things together and started to get to her feet. "None of my business, but I couldn't help seeing. Sorry."

More to put her at her ease again than for any other reason I picked up *The Times* and showed it to her. "I was trying, you see. A Hebridean island—it does sound like a place where one could work in peace, and they have actually called it an ivory tower. There, I've ringed it."

She read the advertisement aloud, then looked up, bright-eyed. "Mull? An island off Mull? You've answered this?"

"I was thinking of it."

"Well, isn't that something? Ann Tracy and I are going to Mull this summer. Two weeks. She's fixing it up, I've never been, but her people used to spend holidays up there, and she says it can be fabulous, weather and midges permitting. What a co-incidence! It sounds just the thing—like fate, really, after what you were saying. You will answer it, won't you?"

"It looks as if I'd better, doesn't it?" I said. "I'll write this very evening."

But fate had not quite finished with me. That evening my brother Crispin telephoned me.

Crispin is a doctor, a partner in a four-man practice in Petersfield in Hampshire. He is six years older than I am, married, with two children away at school. He would have preferred, I knew, to keep them at home, but Ruth, his wife, had overruled him in that, as she did in quite a few other matters. Not that Crispin was a weak man, but he was a very busy one, and had to be content to leave the management of their joint lives largely to his highly capable wife. They were tolerably happy together, as marriages seem to go, a happiness achieved partly by agreeing to differ.

One thing they differed about was holidays. Ruth loved travel, cities, shops, theatres, beach resorts. Crispin, when on leave from his demanding routine, craved for peace and open spaces. He, like me, loved Scotland, and made for it whenever he got the chance. There he walked and fished and took photographs which later, when he found time, he processed himself in a friend's dark-room. Over the years he had acquired real skill in his hobby, and had exhibited some of his studies of Scottish scenery and wildlife; his real passion was bird photography, and through the years he had

amassed a remarkable collection of pictures. Some of these had been published in
periodicals like *Country Life* and the wildlife
journals, but the best had never been
shown. I knew he had a private hope that
some day he might make a book with them.
When our vacations coincided, we often
holidayed together, content in our respec-
tive solitudes.

So when he rang up that evening to tell
me he was taking a fortnight's leave towards
the end of June and what about a trip north
as soon as term ended, I did feel as if the
fates themselves had taken a hand.

"I'd been planning that very thing." I told
him about the advertisement, and he was
enthusiastic. I let him talk on about harriers
and divers and skuas and all the rare and
marvellous birds that would no doubt be
waiting around to be photographed, and
then put in the usual cautious query:

"And Ruth?"

"Actually, no, not this time." The usual
casual answer. "She doesn't like the Highlands, you know that, and she's got rather
a lot on just at present. She's planning to
take a holiday abroad later on, after John
and Julie go back to school. But if you can

get this place . . . It could be really good. Most of the young birds will still be at the nest, and if the weather lets us, we might get across to the Treshnish Isles as well. Look, Rose, why not? It sounds great. Why don't you go right ahead and get the details, and then we'll be in touch again?"

And so it was arranged. I wrote that night to the box number.

And got my ivory tower.

CHAPTER 2

The isle of Moila is the first stop past Tobermory. It is not a large island, perhaps nine miles by five, with formidable cliffs to the north-west that face the weather rather like the prow of a ship. From the steep sheep-bitten turf at the head of these cliffs the land slopes gently down towards a glen where the island's only sizable river runs seawards out of a loch cupped in a shallow basin among low hills. Presumably the loch—lochan, rather, for it is not large—is fed by springs eternally replenished by the rain, for nothing flows into it except small burns seeping through rush and bog myrtle, which spread after storm into sodden quag-mires of moss. But the outflow is perennially full, white water pouring down to where the moor cleaves open and lets it fall to sea.

The island's coast is mainly rocky, but, except for the northerly crags, the coastal cliffs are low, thrusting out here and there into the sea to enclose small curved beaches. Most of these are shingle beaches, but those facing west are sandy, the white shell sand of the Atlantic shore, backed by the machair, that wonderful wild grassland of the west coast, which in May and June is filled with flowers and all the nesting birds that any photographer could wish for.

When I first saw Moila it was on a beautiful day in the last week of June. My term had ended a few days before the start of Crispin's leave, so we had agreed to travel up separately, and meet on Moila itself. The island ferry, as I had discovered, sailed three times a week, on Mondays, Wednesdays, and Saturdays; it went from Oban to Tobermory on the Isle of Mull, and then called at Moila on its way to Coll and Tiree. I had also discovered that there would be little, if any, use for a car on Moila, so both my brother and I had arranged to travel up by train.

It was a pleasant journey. I took the night train for Fort William, which stops at Crianlarich at seven in the morning. With a three-hour wait there, I ate a large breakfast, did a quarter of the day's crossword, then boarded the little local train that runs through Glen Lochy and past the northern end of Loch Awe, to finish at Oban on the west coast. The ferry for the outer isles was due to leave at six on the following morning, so I checked into the waterfront hotel where I had booked, then spent the day exploring Oban, and went to bed early. At half past five next morning I boarded the ferry, and was on the final stage of my journey.

The sea was calm, and Oban, caught in the clear light of a summer morning, looked charming and toylike, as we sailed sedately out between the islets and castle-crowned rocks, with sea-birds drifting in our wake, and everywhere, even over the smell of salt and wind, the scents of summer. Idyllic. Just the setting for an ivory tower.

Or so I still hoped. Nobody I had spoken to in the train, or on the ferry, had ever visited Moila, which must support, so I was told by one slow-spoken Highlander, no more than thirty folk in all.

"So you'll be right back to nature, and let us hope that the natives are friendly." The twinkle in his eye was reassuring, but when we tied up at Tobermory and the purser

pointed out to sea where a group of small
rocks (or so it seemed) showed strung out
on the horizon like a mother duck with her
ducklings after her, I felt a cowardly twinge,
and found myself wondering what the "relatively mod cons" could be.

"Yon big island, see? That's Moila," said
my guide.

"And the others?"

"Och, they've all got names, but I could
not tell you what they are. There's no folk
there, only the birds."

"Can you get to them?"

"Oh, aye, with a bit of luck, on a fine day.
Parties do go out, folk with cameras to film
the birds. You're one of these bird-watchers,
are you?"

"Not really But my brother's very keen.
He's coming to join me later this week. Do
you know if we'll be able to hire a boat in
Moila?"

But here he had to leave me to attend to
stores which were being brought on board,
and some twenty minutes later I could see
the place for myself.

The ferry was not big, but she dwarfed the
harbour—she had to stand off from the jetty

and land us by boat—and indeed the village. As far as I could see, there were some eight or nine cottages strung out on a narrow road which circled the bay The building nearest the jetty was the post office-cum-shop. A homemade notice informed me that it was kept by M. McDougall, who also did bed and breakfasts. Some fifty yards away was a white-washed building surrounded by a stretch of asphalt; the village school, I was to discover, where on alternate Sundays the minister from Tobermory came over to hold a service. A narrow river, little more than a stream, lapsed gently over its stones past the post office. It was spanned by a narrow hump-backed bridge of the picturesque variety that is guaranteed to damage any car that uses it. But, as I had been warned, there were no cars. One battered LandRover stood outside the post office, and leaning against the school-house wall were a couple of bicycles. No other forms of transport. Nor, as far as I could see, did the road continue beyond the end of the village.

And my cottage, I had been informed, lay at the other side of the island.

Well, I had asked for it. I left my cases

parked on the quay, and made my way into the post office.

Since the thrice-weekly visit of the ferry brought all the island's mail and supplies, and the post office was very small, the place was crowded, and the post-mistress, busily sorting through a pile of mail and newspapers, while exchanging two days' news in Gaelic with the ferry's master, had no glance to spare for me. The little shop had been arranged as what I have seen described as a mini-supermarket, so I found a basket and busied myself with collecting what supplies I thought I might need for the next couple of days. I was called to myself by the echoing hoot of the ferry's siren, to find that the shop had emptied of its crowd, and the post-mistress, taking off her spectacles, was hurrying round to the store counter to look after the stranger.

"You'll be the young lady for Camus na Dobhrain? Miss Fenemore, was it?"

She was a thinnish woman of perhaps fifty, with greying hair carefully arranged, and very blue eyes. She wore a flowered smock, and her spectacles hung round her neck on a cord. She had the beautiful skin of the islands, with hardly a wrinkle, except

near the eyes, where the smile lines puck-
ered the corners. She was not smiling now,
but her look was full of a benevolent curiosity, and the soft island voice, with the lilt
of the Gaelic moving through it like a gentle
sea-swell, warmed me as palpably as if the
sun had come into the dim and cluttered
little shop.

"Yes, I'm Rose Fenemore. And you are
Mrs. McDougall? How do you do?" We
shook hands. "And yes, I'm for the cottage
that the Harris Agency advertised. Is that the
one? I don't understand Gaelic, I'm afraid."

"And how should you? Yes, indeed, that
is the one. The English for it is 'Otters' Bay'
It is the only place on Moila that is to let.
We're not just a metropolis, as you see."
She smiled, busying herself with my pur-
chases as she spoke. "You'll not have been
here before, then? Well, if the weather stays
fine you'll find plenty of nice walks, and I'm
told that the house at Otters' Bay is comfortable enough these days. But lonely. You
are by yourself, are you?"

"Till Wednesday, at least. My brother's
hoping to come then." I gave her all she
wanted to know. I was part of the week's
news, after all. "He's a doctor, from Hamp-

shire. He couldn't get away when I did, so I came up on my own. Does the Wednesday ferry come in at the same time?"

"It does. You have not put any firelighters in. You will find it is much easier to get your fire going with one of those. Are you used to a peat fire?"

"No, but I'm hoping I can learn. Mrs. McDougall, how do I get from here to the cottage? I'm told it's about two miles. I can easily walk to do shopping and so on, but I've got a couple of suitcases here now, and I certainly can't manage those."

"No worry about that. I saw your cases there, and Archie McLaren will have them into the Land-Rover by this time. So will you perhaps be wanting a couple of bags, say, of coal to help with the fire? The house will be dry enough; there was a couple in it through the middle of May, and we have had good weather, but you would be better to stock up now for what next week might bring."

"Yes, of course. Thank you very much. Two bags of coal, then, please, and the fire-lighters, and—yes, I think I've remembered everything else. Oh, about milk and bread.

Can one only get it fresh when the ferry comes over?"

"We have fresh milk here from the farm, but you would be better to take some of the long-life with you. It's a long walk from Otters' Bay in the bad weather. Here it is. Two cartons, and it will keep a long time, even with no fridge. I don't know if you have one over there. . . . The bread comes with the boat. Will I keep you a loaf on Wednesday? And another at the weekend, or two then, perhaps? Mostly we make our own if we want it fresh. There, is that everything?"

"I think so, thank you. How much is that, Mrs. McDougall?"

She told me, and I paid her. A young man, dark, short, burly, in a navy guernsey and jeans and gumboots, came in and lifted the coal bags into the Land-Rover beside my cases. I picked up the carrier bag where the post-mistress had packed my groceries.

"I don't imagine there's a telephone at the cottage, is there?"

"There is not. There is one here, and one at the House, and that is all there are. And the one at the House is cut off since the old lady died."

"The House?" Somehow, the way she said it gave it a capital letter.

"The big house. It's not far from you, half a mile along the shore, maybe. Taigh na Tuir, they call it. That means House of the Tower. There is a small island off the coast just there, with the remains of a broch on it. I suppose that is the tower that the House was named for. It was built as a shooting-lodge in the old days, and then the Hamiltons bought it, and lived there most summers, but old Mrs. Hamilton, she was the last of them, died this February, so it's empty now, and likely to stay so." She smiled. "It's not everyone wants the kind of peace and quiet we have on Moila."

"I can imagine. Well, I'm all set to enjoy it, anyway And I don't really want a phone, except to make sure about my brother's coming. So I'll walk over here tomorrow and telephone him, if I may. What time do you shut?"

"Half past five, but if you want the telephone, then come to the house door. No, it's no trouble, it's what everyone does, and the cheap calls are after six anyway. Just you come. That's it, then." She picked up the second carrier bag and saw me to the door with it. "Archie will see you into the house, and if there's anything more that you need, you will let him know. And I'll look for you maybe tomorrow. Goodbye. Look after the lady, now, Archie."

Archie was understood to say that he would. I got in beside him, and we set off. The Land-Rover had seen better days, and once we had left the village street and taken to the track—it was little more—that wound up from the village towards the moorland, conversation was difficult. After one or two tries, met by a nod or a noncommittal noise from Archie, I gave up, and looked about me.

I suppose that there are very few places on Moila from which one cannot see the sea. The track, rough and strewn with stones, climbed, at first gently, through sheep-cropped turf bristling with reeds and thistles and islanded with stretches of bracken. Once we were out of sight of the village there were no trees except, here and there, thorns dragged sideways by the wind and shorn close by the weather. The track grew steeper, and twisted. Now to either hand was heather, at this season still dark and flowerless, except where patches of the early bell-heather splashed their vivid purple

across grey rock. The whins, those perpet-
ual wonders, were blazing gold, and everywhere over the stretches of grass between
the bracken spread the tiny white and yellow
flowers of lady's bedstraw and tormentil.
The very lichen patching the grey rocks was
bright mustard-gold, like flowers. Away to
the right I saw the flat gleam of the loch.

Nothing could be heard above the noise
of the engine, but I saw a lark spring sky-
wards out of the heather, and another, a few
minutes later, sink to its rest. A pair of grey-
backed crows—hooded crows—flew across
the track, and then, as the Land-Rover
topped the rise and started down into a narrowing glen, a buzzard soared up in leisurely
circles, to be lost over the crest of the moor.

Then we were running gently downhill beside a burn, towards the distant gleam of
the sea. Here, in the shelter that the glen
gave from the Atlantic gales, the trees
crowded close, and reasonably tall. Oaks,
mostly, but there were beeches and ash
trees, with birch and hazel everywhere, tan-
gled with brambles and wild honeysuckle.
Along the edge of the burn were thickets of
alder and hawthorn standing knee-deep in
fox-gloves.

The track levelled out, the glen widened, and there below us was the bay.

Otters' Bay was very small, a pebbled crescent backed by a storm beach of smooth boulders. Thick black curves of dry seaweed marked the reach of the tides. To our left a high cliff cut off the view, and to the right a lowish headland jutted well out into the sea. Narrowing my eyes against the Atlantic glitter I could see the line of a path that climbed from the bay and on over the headland to the west. And beyond the crest of the headland, hazy with distance, the shape of a hill, smooth and symmetrical, like a drawn-up knee.

Then the Land-Rover came to a halt beside a rough jetty made of stacked boulders tied down with fencing wire, and there, backed against the cliff a short way above us, was the cottage.

CHAPTER 3

The cottage was bigger than I had expected. Originally it had been built on the
usual pattern, a tiny square hallway, with
doors to either side leading into the two
"front" rooms, and a steep enclosed stair
up to the twin bedrooms under the pitch of
the roof. But someone, fairly recently, had
done a job of conversion; the two downstairs rooms were thrown into one, with the
staircase half dividing them. The sitting-
room, to the right, had a pleasant fireplace,
and was adequately, if not well, furnished
with a couple of easy chairs, a low table,
and a doubtful-looking sofa pushed back
against the staircase wall. The "kitchen-
diner" on the other side boasted the usual
cupboards and what looked like homemade worktops, and a table near the win-

dow with four chairs drawn up to it. On the worktop stood an electric kettle and a toaster, and these were the only "mod cons" to be seen.

A door at the rear led to a narrow room which ran the width of the cottage and had originally been the "back kitchen" or scullery and wash-house. Under one window was a modern sink and draining-board, with an electric water-heater fixed to the wall above it. Beside this stood the cooker, installed, apparently, by someone who distrusted the island's electricity supply; it was a gas cooker, and had been placed there to be within easy reach of the cylinders of Calor gas that stood just outside the window under a lean-to, beside a stack of peat. That was as far as modernization had gone: the other end of the scullery was just as it had always been, with the old deep sink for laundry, served by a single, presumably cold tap, and in the corner beyond it the copper for "the boil." A deep cupboard, clean and empty, would serve as a storeroom; another, beside the copper, held cleaning tools. No fridge, but the place would be cool even in summer; those windows never saw the sun. Peering out, I could see that there must have been a garden or kail-yard between the cottage and the cliff; now the tumbledown wall enclosed nothing but a tangle of brambles and wild roses almost hiding a garden hut. Alongside the wall a narrow path wound between waist-high nettles to a small structure whose function one could guess at. The house agent had assured me that a bathroom and lavatory had been installed upstairs above the scullery; looking at those nettles, I hope he had told the truth.

"I will take your cases upstairs for you," said Archie McLaren.

"No, don't bother—well, thank you very much."

I dumped the carrier bags of groceries on the kitchen table and started to unpack them. I heard him moving about upstairs, and it was a minute or two before he came down again.

"I was just"—he pronounced it "chust"— "taking a look. She had Robert McDougall over from Mull last year to do the bedrooms up. That is Mary McDougall's cousin from Dervaig. He always does a good job. I had not seen the upstairs rooms since they were finished, but I remember the job they had with the bathroom, and with this." He looked about him with interest. "It was very different here when the family had it. It was Alastair Mackay lived here, that was the gardener at the House. They only moved away two years ago, to the mainland, and then Mrs. Hamilton did the place up for letting. When they took the old oven out, I brought the cooker down myself, and the fittings for the kitchen units. The timber and the bath and such came across by boat into the bay there, and a fine job they had dragging them up to the house."

"I hadn't realized that the cottage be-longs—belonged?—to Mrs. Hamilton. Mrs. McDougall told me that she had died re-cently."

"That is so. She was a nice lady, and when her husband was alive he was a great one for the shooting and the fishing, though there is not much fishing here on Moila. He used to go north for the salmon every year, to the mainland, but she would stay here. She liked it, and then after Colonel Hamilton died she never went away at all, even in the winter. But this last winter was too much for her, poor lady."

"What do you suppose will happen to the House—the big house, I mean—now?"

"I do not know. I think that there is a re-
lation abroad somewhere, but that is all. It
will be sold, I think, but who will buy it?"

"Someone who loves peace and quiet, I
expect."

"An ivory tower?"

I had been reaching up to put packets
and tins into one of the wall cupboards, but
this startled me into turning. "A what?"

"Ivory tower. It was what Mrs. Hamilton
used to say. She was a writer, a real one
who got books printed. When she was
younger she used to write books for children. She said it was a poetic way of saying
you wanted to be left alone."

"I see. Yes, I see. I did wonder. House
agents aren't usually poets."

"What is that?"

"Only that the house agents called it that
when they advertised it. Rather clever of
them. That's what caught my eye. I wonder
if they'll try to sell the cottage too, or if they'll
go on letting it?"

"It has only ever been let in the summer,
and no one has been here yet this year except the people last month, folk from Corn-
wall, I think. They came with a boat, and did

all their shopping in Tobermory, so we did not see much of them at all."

"I suppose a boat would make sense if one was here for long. Do you have a boat?"

"I do. If you should ever want to go fishing, or maybe to take a look at the bird islands, you will just let me know?"

"I certainly will. Oh, I nearly forgot. Did you unload the coal?"

"I did. It is out the back where the peat is kept. Just beside the door. Will I get some in for you now? No bother. Do you know how to make a fire with the peats?"

"Mrs. McDougall asked me that," I said. "I don't know. I can but try. I might have to ask for help with that as well."

"You will be welcome. But you will find plenty of kindling and dry wood down on the beach. Then give the peats plenty of air. If once you get it going, it is a good fire."

"I'll do my best. Thanks very much, Archie. Now, what do I owe you?"

I paid him and he took his leave, but in the doorway he hesitated, then suddenly, as if the question had forced itself out in spite of good manners, asked: "Are you sure you will be all right here, all on your own? What are you going to do? It's a lonely spot, and if it's walking you want, Moila is such a small island, and once you have been round it, you have seen it all. There is nothing special about Moila, except maybe the birds on the outer islands, and they will be away soon."

I smiled. "I wanted an ivory tower. I'm a writer, too, you see."

"Well, now . . . A writer, is it? Yes, I do see." His tone and look said, clearly, that everything—any possible lunacy—was now fully explained.

I laughed. "I don't intend to write all the time, though there is some work I want to do. But I'm not really planning to be a hermit; my brother's coming over soon, and I know he'll want to go to the islands, so we'll be in touch. Thanks again."

I watched the Land-Rover grind its way up the track till a turn of the glen hid it from sight, and in a few more moments the sound of its engine had faded to silence.

Silence? The wash of waves on the pebbled beach, the crying and calling of the wheeling gulls, the silver chain of sound from a lark above the cliff-top, and, as a final coda, the distant, breathy note of the ferry's siren as she drew away towards the west.

The last link gone. Solitude. Complete and unassailable solitude.

I shut the front door gently, a symbolic gesture which shut out what sounds there were, and went upstairs to see what that nice lady, Mrs. Hamilton, had provided in the way of beds.

The beds were reasonable, the bedrooms tiny, tucked under the slope of the roof, and charming, with white paint, flowery wallpaper, a minimum of furniture, and of course that marvellous view right out to the south-west. Storm-direction, I supposed, and spared a thought for the winter; but in June, surely, all would be well? The windows were tightly shut, and the rooms smelled stuffy, but not damp, though the drawers of the chest stuck as I tried to pull them open. The solitary ornament in my room was a faded copy of a biblical scene by Gustave Doré, sinners drowning in a rough sea. Rather too pertinent, I thought, for the place's original dweller, who must have gone down to the Atlantic in a small boat on many a stormy night. But today the real sea looked wonderful, silken, with a gentle running glitter where the tide moved, and here and there

the tilt and flash of white wings in the sunlight as the gulls sailed out from the cliffs.

It would do. It would do very well. I would
finish unpacking, have a look at the cooker
and set things ready for supper, then I would
take a walk out to look at the sea, and gather
kindling in case the evening turned chilly
enough for a fire.

There was, as Archie had promised,
plenty of good kindling among the piled jet-
sam on the beach. I soon had an armful,
then clambered up off the shingle to the better walking of the salt-washed turf where the
burn, dividing into deep peaty runnels, cut
its way to the shore. Sea-pinks were thick
everywhere, with here and there patches of
small shingle glistening with broken shells.
An oyster-catcher screamed from somewhere at the end of the beach, warning its
young. Not far away I caught, from the corner of my eye, the flickering movement as
a ringed plover scudded and ran among the
sea-pinks. It went silently, dodging and hiding; it must have left its nest at my approach.

Any thought I may have had about finding
the nest for Crispin's camera left me then.
Gradually, over the last few minutes, I had

become conscious of a growing discomfort, a tickling, burning sensation in the face and hands, and even in my hair a stinging sort of unpleasantness that suddenly became insupportable.

Midges. I had forgotten about the midges. The curse of the Highlands. The infinitesimal and unbeatable enemy The serpent in paradise.

Tucking my load of sticks under one arm, and rubbing my free hand hard over face and hair, I scurried for the safety of the cottage.

After all, the evening stayed mild, so the fire never got lit. I made and ate supper, washed up, then watched the changing view of evening from the haven of the cottage window, and went early to bed.

CHAPTER 4

I awoke next morning to a brilliant pearly light, but when I went to the window, no sea was visible. Nothing, in fact, was visible. The world was shrouded in a curtain of mist. This was not the sort of fog one is used to in towns, but a veil of salt-smelling white, damp and mild, with all the soft brilliance of a thin curtain drawn between earth and sun. But view there was none. I could not even see as far as the mouth of the burn. So, no walk today, until I was a little more certain of my way. Even the main track to the village could be treacherous in this blinding, moveless white.

I was not disappointed. I told myself so firmly, several times. I had all that I had wanted, peace and privacy, a day to myself before Crispin came, and an absolute com-

pulsion to stay indoors and take another
look at the poem that had been broken into
by the tutorial in Cambridge. I would look
at it again, and see if it had been totally de-
stroyed. At least no person from Porlock
was likely to interrupt me today.

No one did. The day went by, still and
silent but for the muted calling of the sea-
birds, and the sad little pipe of the ringed
plover on the shingle. I sat at the kitchen
table, staring at the blind white blankness
in front of me, and slowly, like a clear spring
welling up from the common earth, the
poem rose and spread and filled me, un-
stoppable as flood water, technique unknot-
ting even as it ran, like snags rolled away
on the flood. When it comes, it is worth everything in the world. There is too much
easy talk about "inspiration," but at such
times one sees it exactly for what it is, a
breathing in of all experience, all apprehen-
sion of beauty, all love. As a fire needs air
to make it burn, so a poem needs to be
fuelled by each one of these. And the great-
est of these is love.

When I looked up at last, it was to see the
near cliffs bright with the afternoon sun, and
the sea creaming calmly against the storm

beach in the gentlest of high tides. The horizon was still invisible, but above the line of mist that hid it, the sky was clear, with the promise of a lovely evening. An evening with a breeze; I could see movement in the bracken that edged the track, and cloud-shadows moved from time to time over the sea-pinks. So much for the midges, and it would be better at the head of the track and over the central moors. I would make myself some tea, I decided as I packed away my papers, then walk over to the post office to make my call to Crispin.

My sister-in-law answered the telephone, in the voice which, whether she means it or not, always sounds abrasive and resentful when she speaks to me. She was sorry, but Crispin was out on call. No, she did not know when he would be home. When did she ever? His train? Well, it now seemed that there was someone he wanted to see in Glasgow, so he was taking this chance to fit that in. He had booked on tomorrow night's sleeper, and would head up to Oban on Friday. Then, she gathered, he would get the ferry the next morning, Saturday. Would that be right?

"It could be. I was hoping he'd manage tomorrow's boat, but Saturday would be great. I've found out more about it now, so if you wouldn't mind giving him a message, Ruth? Have you got a pencil handy? Well, the ferry is the one for Coll and Tiree . . . C.O.L.L. and T.I.R.E.E . . . Yes, they're two of the islands in the Inner Hebrides; Crispin will know. It leaves at six in the morning, and they want you on board soon after half past five. I stayed at the Columba Hotel, just near the quay. I'll make a reservation for him for Friday night. Oh, and tell him that Moila's too small for the ferry to dock, so he'll come ashore in a boat. I won't offer to meet the ferry—it docks at eight in the morning—but I'll arrange transport for him to the cottage. Did you get all that?"

"Yes. But wouldn't it be better if I got him to call you back when he comes in?"

I laughed. "It would be difficult. There's only the public phone in the post office, and I've just walked two miles to get to that. But I'll give you the number"—I gave it—"and if he wants to leave a message for me, Mrs. McDougall will take it."

"Mrs. McDougall. Yes." Now it was her professional voice, quick and cool, the doctor's wife taking another message down. Then she was herself again. "Rose, what's it like? Two miles from the phone? And you had to walk it? I must say, it sounds just the sort of place Crispin would love."

"He would. He will. It's quite lovely." I added, in total insincerity: "You really ought to have come, Ruth. The cottage is tiny, but it's charming, and the views are out of this world."

"But what on earth would there be to *do*?"

"Well, nothing." Nothing, blessed state for the hard-working Crispin, and for myself after the turmoil of exams and end of term.

"I," said my sister-in-law, who never, I am sure, means to be offensive, "simply cannot stand being idle. I'm going to Marrakesh in September. Marvellous hotel, bags of sunshine, and plenty of tours and fascinating shopping."

"That sounds wonderful. Enjoy it. I'll have to go now, Ruth. I'll ring again on Thursday evening to see if Crispin's going to make it. Goodbye now."

"Goodbye." And she rang off.

Mrs. McDougall was in her kitchen taking a batch of bread out of the oven. I paid her for the call, and stayed chatting for a while, answering her queries about the cottage and then telling her of my brother's expected arrival, and the possibility that he might telephone with a message.

"I expect I'll walk over this way every day anyway, and if he does come on Saturday, could Archie be here, please, to take him down with his bags to the cottage?"

"He will be here. He always meets the boat. There are always goods to carry that have been ordered. Well, it will be nice for you to have your brother here, and we will hope for the best. I am afraid that there is bad weather forecast. I have just heard it on the news."

"Oh, dear, is there? Really bad? Enough to stop the ferry crossing?"

"It has to be very bad indeed for that. Don't worry, your brother will get here. But you might find the cottage a bit drafty if it gets really rough."

"I'll batten down the hatches," I told her. She laughed, and we talked for a few minutes longer. When I left I had a bottle of midge repellent in my pocket, and a loaf of new bread, still warm, in a plastic carrier.

The loaf was a gift. The natives were friendly, after all.

I went slowly, and presently found myself walking towards a most spectacular sunset. Gold, scarlet and blazing flame I had seen before, but never like this, washing over the low clouds from below, and backed by the most delicate and limpid green which faded to primrose and then into the shadowy greys of the upper sky.

I stood to watch. To my right was the small loch, edged with deep reedy banks of moss and thymy turf. The water lay smooth as glass, polished with all the colours of the sunset sky Then something moved, and the shining world broke up into arrowing ripples, as a bird slid across the water, no more than a shape of black against the glare. A duck? Too big. A diver? It was possible. I had never seen one, but my brother had talked of them, and I knew that he was hoping he might find one here. As I screwed up my eyes against the dazzle, trying to see the creature so that I might describe it to Crispin, it vanished. Duck or diver, it had dived, and, though I waited for long minutes, it did not appear again. I walked on, and down the hill towards the cottage which, already, seemed like home.

It is never quite dark on a clear June night in the Highlands. And never, in the long light nights, do the sea-birds cease from calling and flying. I went outside again that night, just before bed-time, to look at the stars. Back in the city, or in fact anywhere that I had lived, the night sky was disfigured by street-lamps and the city's emanations. But here, in a dear arch of pewter-grey air, the stars were low and bright and as thick as daisies on a lawn. I picked out the Big Dipper, and Orion, and the Pleiades, and of course the long splashing trail of the Milky Way, but that was as far as my knowledge went. Of one thing I could be certain; the weather was changing. A wind was getting up, and even as I stood there, the lower stars were obscured by drifting darkness. The cries of the sea-birds, muted, seemed to change, too. And the soft murmur of the sea. It was perceptibly colder, and the wind smelt of rain.

I went indoors and to bed.

During the night the wind got up, and the morning dawned grey and blustery, with bursts of heavy rain. Thankful that I had taken the trouble to gather dry wood while it was fine, I lighted the fire, and soon had a cheerful blaze going.

And, once the chores were done, there was nothing to do but write.

It is time, I think, to make a confession. Though I was a student of literature, and, I believe, a reasonably good teacher, and loved my work, and though I was, moreover, a serious poet who had gained some small recognition in circles even outside my own University, my writing life was not confined to poems and articles, or even lectures. I wrote science fiction.

Not only wrote it, but published it and made what seemed to a poorly paid lecturer to be a very acceptable amount of money with it. Under another name, of course. The flights of Hugh Templar's imagination paid Rose Fenemore very well indeed. They also gave her a much valued safety-valve for an almost too-active imagination. The pure invention of these tales, the exercise of what at its best can be called the high imagination, allow the writer (in Dryden's phrase) to take the clogs off his fancy, and to escape the world at will.

So through that dismal day Hugh Templar sat at his kitchen table and pursued the adventures of a team of space-travellers who had discovered a world directly behind the sun, which was a mirror-image of our own Earth, with the same physical composition, but with a rather different kind of population, a race having strange and, I hoped, thought-provoking ideas about how to run their planet . . .

At ten o'clock the lights went out.

Though normally, in the Highlands, there is almost enough light at that time to write by, the storm-clouds that had thickened and threatened all day made it quite dark. The fire had died to cold ashes, but I felt my way to where I had seen a candlestick, left ready on the mantelpiece, presumably as insurance against just this event. I crossed to the uncurtained window and peered out. The wind was stronger than ever, and fistfuls of rain hurtled against the glass. A wild and nasty night.

I finished the section I had been writing—an idea left in mid-paragraph tends to vanish very quickly—then took myself and my candle early to bed.

* * *

The walls of the cottage were thick enough to shut out the worst sounds of the storm's buffeting, and even the creaking of doors and rattling of windows could not keep me awake for long. But something, some sharper, un-accustomed sound, brought me out of my first deep sleep into listening wakefulness.

The storm was still raging, more fiercely now than before. I could hear the crash of waves on the shingle, and the intermittent shriek of the wind as it tore through the gaps in the kail-yard wall.

But the sound that had startled me awake was different. It came from within the cot-tage, a quiet sound, but cutting through all the noise from outside. The closing of a door; the back door, I thought. And then sounds from the scullery. A tap running, and the echo of metal as the kettle was filled.

Crispin? Against all expectation, all pos-sibility, had my brother managed to make his way here, and cross to Moila in spite of the storm?

Too bewildered by sleep to think just how impossible that was, I slid out of bed, pulled on my slippers, threw my dressing-gown on, and opened my bedroom door. There was a light on downstairs, and as my bedroom door opened, all sounds ceased from inside the house. For a moment I thought I had been mistaken, and that perhaps I had left the switch on after the light failed, but no, I was sure I had switched off. And I had locked the back door. I ran downstairs.

He was just turning from the sink, kettle in hand. A young man, tallish, slenderly built, with dark hair dragged into a tousle by the wind, and a narrow, pale-skinned face. A good-looking face; blue eyes, straight nose, cheeks flushed with cold and wet with rain, and with tomorrow's stubble already showing dark. He wore a navy fisherman's jersey and gumboots, and a heavy anorak, shiny and running with wet.

I had never seen him before in my life.

I stopped dead in the doorway. He stood, rigid, gripping the kettle.

We both spoke at the same time, and, inevitably, the same words.

"Who the hell are you?"

CHAPTER 5

He set the kettle down with a rap on the draining-board. He seemed even more taken aback than I was, and this heartened me. I said, with a reasonable show of calmness: "You're welcome, of course, to take shelter from the storm, but do you usually walk into someone else's house without knocking? Or did you knock, and I didn't hear you? I thought the door was locked, anyway."

"Your house?" He asked it without any apparent sense of its being a stupid question.

"Well, yes. Temporarily, anyway. I've rented it for a fortnight. Oh, I see. You know the owners? And you thought you could just walk in—"

"As a matter of fact, I thought it was my

own house. I was brought up here. See?" He put a hand in a pocket and brought out a key, the duplicate of the one I had been given, which fitted both front and back doors. "I'd no idea the place had changed hands. I'm sorry."

"I'm sorry, too." An awkward silence. He stood by the sink, dripping quietly onto the scullery matting. He showed no sign of offering to go, and, hearing the wind outside hurling fistfuls of rain about, I could hardly blame him. I cleared my throat. "Well, this is a bit awkward, isn't it? The people who lived here moved away a couple of years ago, so I was told. I don't know where they went, but Mrs. McDougall at the post office could probably tell you, if you wanted to get in touch again. I think she said the name was Mackay."

"That is right." Now in his voice I could hear, through the flattening cosmopolitan overlay, the unmistakable lilt of the islands. "My father used to do the garden at Taigh na Tuir. My foster-father, that is."

"You mean your *parents* lived here? Then this was your home?"

"That is right," he said again.

"Well . . ." I stopped, at a loss for words.

He smiled then for the first time, and the smile lightened his face to a sudden, vivid charm.

"A bit of a facer, isn't it? For me, too."

"You mean you really didn't know they'd left? You just let yourself into your own home and thought they'd be upstairs asleep?"

"Just that."

"But—but that's awful! You . . ." I stopped again. There was really nothing left to say. I finished, feebly: "You're taking it very calmly. What will you do?"

"What can I do, but wait till morning?" The smile was still there, but behind it now was a hint of trouble, and more than a hint of tiredness. "It wasn't quite such a shock as you might think. It certainly shook me when you came downstairs, but then I just thought my people might be away, and have let the cottage. Then I thought . . . well, as it happens, I did know that the old lady— Mrs. Hamilton—had died earlier this year, and of course that could have meant that Dad's job had packed up and they'd had to move. But then, when you said they'd been gone for a couple of years . . ." He paused and took his breath in. No smile now. He frowned down for a few moments at the damp patch on the matting at his feet, then he shook his head, as if ridding himself of some unwelcome thought, and looked up at me again. "In fact, that's still what may have happened, isn't it? If she hadn't been well, perhaps, for some time, and had lost interest in the garden, and wanted to get the cottage done over for sale or letting, then she might have told them to go?"

He finished on a note of inquiry, but I shook my head. "I wouldn't know. I've only just got here, and I really haven't heard anything more than I told you. But how does it happen that you didn't know they were leaving? All that time ago—did they never write?"

"I've been abroad. Moving around, and one loses touch, I'm afraid. I've only just got back to the U.K." He looked around him. "I did notice the changes, of course, but I just thought the old lady had had the house done over for them—the parents. But she must have done it after they left; she'd have to, if she wanted to let the place. It wasn't much before, you can see." A glance at the corner where the copper stood, then at the doorway behind me, where the light fell on the gleaming worktops and new cupboards.

He lifted his shoulders and let them fall in a dismissive shrug. "Ah, well, I can see now, they've made a pretty good job of it. I didn't really stop to look earlier—I was just so glad to get out of the weather."

"I can imagine. You said you knew that Mrs. Hamilton had died?"

"As it happens, yes. I hired my boat on Faarsay—that's a little island south of Mull— and they'd heard about Mrs. Hamilton, but they didn't know my folks, so no one told me our house was let."

"I—yes, I see. Well, I'm sorry you had to find out this way."

A pause. There seemed to be nothing else to say The water dripped steadily from his anorak to make a puddle on the floor. He looked pale and, I thought, tired and rather lost. I said crisply: "Give me the kettle. You look as if you could do with a hot drink, and as a matter of fact, so could I." I carried the kettle into the other room, plugged it in, and switched on. "What'll you have? Coffee? Tea? Cocoa? I'm not stocked up with strong drink yet, I'm afraid. Why don't you take that wet anorak off and get the fire going again while I make the drinks?"

He did as I suggested, dropping the wet

clothes into a corner by the back door. "Well, God bless this house. It's very good of you to take it like this. I'm sorry if I gave you a fright. The coal's still kept just outside the back door?"

"Yes, but I brought some in earlier; it's in that bucket there, and there's peat there, too, and it's dry. I suppose you're used to peat fires? You can show me how. Are you sure cocoa will do?"

"If there's coffee, I'd rather have that, please. Yes, instant would be fine. Thanks." He came in from the scullery with the coal bucket in one hand and in the other a fat metal cylinder. "I'll certainly show you, but didn't you know about this?"

"Don't tell me it's a gas poker? How wonderful! Where was it?"

"At the back of the cupboard. We hardly ever used it, but it's a great standby, and very quick." He dumped the cylinder down by the sitting-room hearth and knelt to stack peat and coal over the cold core of the fire. The kettle boiled and I made the drinks and followed him through to set the mugs down on the low table near the fireplace.

"Do you take sugar? Will that really burn?"

"Yes, please. Yes, indeed, given time, it will burn well. This always was a good fire. They have changed the fireplace, but the chimney will be the same, and it burns hot. You will see."

"Incidentally, were you hoping to get a meal here? Because I'm afraid that all I've got at the moment—"

"No, no, that's OK. The drink will do fine. I've got this to help it, anyway." He took the mug I handed him, then produced a flask from his pocket, and tipped a generous measure into his mug. He held the flask out to me, but I shook my head. The fire caught the peat and spread into a warming glow. Feeling as if I was still asleep and having a very curious dream, I settled myself on the other side of the hearth from the stranger and took a sip of cocoa. It is a simple drink, but wonderfully heartening.

"My name's Rose Fenemore," I said, "and I'm from Cambridge."

"Mine's Ewen Mackay, from Moila, but it's a long, long time since I was here. You're taking this very well, Rose Fenemore. Some women would have come downstairs with the poker at the ready."

"I might have done, only I'm expecting

my brother to join me, I don't quite know when. I was too sleepy to wonder how he'd managed, at this time of night." I glanced at the window. "Did you really bring a boat across tonight in that?"

"Why not? Rounding the Horn is worse." He laughed. "As a matter of fact, the really nasty bit was when I was walking across here, coming over the head of the cliff there with the wind trying to blow me out to sea again."

"Over the cliff? The headland? Then you didn't put into the bay here?"

"No. With the wind and the tide this way, it's too tricky to bring a boat in here. There's a little cove about half way between here and the big house—the Hamilton house. It's a safe mooring in any weather, and the nearest to home."

The last word fell queerly in the little room, with the fire burning cozily and the insistent sounds of the storm at the window. I sipped cocoa, and wondered how and when I would be able to turn him out into the night again. Or even if. The windows, black as pitch, were streaming with water, and from time to time doors and windows rattled as if the cottage were under attack. I would not have put a stray dog out into such a night.

And the man, apparently, still regarded the place as "home." Well, Rose Fenemore, now might be the time to broaden your outlook a little. I could name at least three of my friends who would have been prompt to offer this undeniably attractive young man a doss-down on the sofa, and one of them who would have already been thinking of taking him upstairs for the night. . . .

He was saying something about the Hamilton house, a question.

"I'm sorry?" I said.

"I asked if you had been over there yet?"

"No."

"You should go. It's quite a good path over the cliff there, and the island with the broch is worth a visit. There's a nice bay there, too, very sheltered. You can take a boat in there most times, except at low water, but it can be awkward then, and in this weather . . . Anyway, I tucked my boat in snugly at Halfway House—the cove—and walked over to Taigh na Tuir. That's what they call the Hamilton place."

"Yes, I know."

"I just wanted to see it again." He reached

forward to turn off the gas poker and add a couple of peats to the fire. "Even though I knew there was no one there. And even if they hadn't told me, I would have known. She never slept well, and she used to read half the night. It seemed queer to me to see the windows all dark and the curtains still not drawn . . . I don't think I believed it till then, that she was gone, I mean. You might say that Taigh na Tuir was as much home to me as this was. More. I was over there most days when I was a boy."

"Mrs. McDougall—no, I think it was Archie McLaren—told me that your father looked after the garden there."

"My foster-father." That emphasis again. "I was adopted. Did they not tell you that? It was never a secret. Yes, he worked at the House, and so did my mother. But they—the Colonel and Mrs. Hamilton—they had no family, only a brother who lived abroad all the time, and, well, they treated me like a son, or grandson, rather. It was the Colonel himself who taught me how to shoot, and I always went with him for the fishing. The way they were with me, I sometimes wondered—"

He broke off. A quick flash of a glance from those blue eyes, then he turned away.

"You wondered?"

"Nothing. Nothing at all . . ." He stirred the peats, the Gaelic suddenly strong in his voice. "But it's a strange feeling to be robbed of both homes all in the same wild night."

Celtic twilight, I thought. Is he dramatizing all this a bit, for sympathy and a bed for the night, or is this the normal way of the Gael? The chill little touch of criticism roused me. Stray dog or no stray dog, I wanted him to go. I sat up in my chair.

"I'm sorry, I really am. But—"

He smiled at me suddenly, the same flash of charm. "And that was not a hint for you to offer me a bed for the night, Miss Rose Fenemore. You've been very kind, and I'm good and dry now, and I've slept on the boat many's the time before, and in worse nights than this. The wind's dropping a bit, anyhow, and she'll be all safe and snug in Halfway House. I'll maybe get round to the harbour in the morning, and have a talk with Mrs. McDougall. Here, let me wash the mugs up for you first."

"No, really, they're nothing. Give me yours."

As I got up to take it from him, there was a sharp rapping at the front door. In the time it took me to turn my head, Ewen Mackay came upright, and a hand moved—incredibly—towards a pocket. It was a movement I had seen a hundred times on television, but never before in real life. For real life, visit Moila, the island of the ivory tower.

His hand dropped. I said, feebly: "Would you answer the door, please? And if it's my brother, don't shoot him."

He didn't smile. He gave me a sideways look that was curiously disconcerting, and went to the door.

It opened on a rush of air. Outside stood a young man in an anorak, the hood blowing back from a soaking tangle of brown hair blackened by the rain, and one hand gripping a duffel bag.

Ewen Mackay stood back for him to enter. "Do come in. The kettle's just on the boil. Mr. Fenemore, I presume?"

The newcomer came in on a gust of the storm. He stood dripping on the rug while Ewen Mackay shut the door behind him. "What?" he asked. He blinked at the light as if it hurt him. His eyes were bloodshot, presumably with the wind, and he looked dazed.

"Your brother made it after all," said Ewen Mackay to me, but I shook my head.

"I've never seen him before in my life," I said.

CHAPTER 6

"I'm terribly sorry to butt in like this." The newcomer looked from Ewen Mackay to me and back again. He was, understandably, taking us for a couple whose holiday idyll he had interrupted, though why we should be sitting by the fire at that hour, with me in a not very elegant dressing-gown and Ewen in stained jeans and a guernsey it would be hard to imagine. Something of the sort was getting through to him. He paused, and finished, uncertainly: "My tent was blown away, and some of my stuff with it. I tried to chase it, but it was no good in the dark, and I went clear into a bog, and in the end I saw your light, so I picked up what was left and came along. If I might just wait here till the storm passes, till daylight, perhaps, and then try again to track my things down?"

"Well, of course," said Ewen Mackay warmly, before I could speak. I looked at him in surprise, but he ignored me. "Come right in and get those wet things off. A shocker, isn't it? We were just having a hot drink. Join us?"

"Thank you. It's good of you. I'd like that." He was shedding his wet things as he spoke, and a glance at me indicated who was supposed to hurry off and get him the hot drink.

I found my voice. I gave Ewen a chilly glance. "If you're the host, you make the drink. You know where the kettle is."

The newcomer looked surprised, but Ewen took it without a blink. In fact, he smiled. "Of course." Then, to the other man: "My name's Mackay, by the way, and this is Rose Fenemore. There's coffee if you'd like it, and it doesn't have to be totally harmless, if you prefer something a bit stronger?"

"Whatever there is. Coffee would be great. Thank you. It's very good of you." He dumped his things on a chair near the door, and came to the fire, hands spread out to the warmth. "My name's Parsons. John Parsons." He spoke over my head to the scullery door, where Ewen was refilling the kettle. He obviously still took us for a couple holidaying together, and his embarrassment at intruding took the form of ignoring my presence.

I was busy wondering why Ewen Mackay, by playing host, had taken such pains to foster that impression. It was hard to see a reason. A stab of male vanity, perhaps? Discovered alone in a remote cottage with a young female whose brother had once described her as "a don, alas, but a dish when she takes the trouble," had he quite deliberately misled the newcomer? Or, to take it further, had he begun to have hopes for the remainder of the night, and so taken this means to get rid of the other man? My own vanity, such as it was, could not accept any of this; in that dressing-gown, and with my hair all over the place, I was hardly something that a chance-met man would want to lay claim to.

"Milk and sugar?" Ewen, still the charming host, was pouring hot water.

Mr. Parsons had turned to stand with his back to the fire, the eternal male hogging the best place in the room. "Great. Yes,

both, thanks." He accepted the steaming
mug from the other man, then addressing
him, and still ignoring me: "Are you on holiday, or do you live here?"

I caught Ewen Mackay's swift glance as
he resumed his place on the other side of
the fireplace. His look was faintly apologetic.
As well it might be, I thought. As an exercise,
even of vanity, it had been pointless. Had
he really thought that I would play along?
Out of sheer curiosity I held my tongue, and
waited.

He stretched out a foot to the fire, stirring
the peats. "I did live here years ago. I was
brought up here. But just at present I'm like
you, an orphan of the storm. Miss Fenemore
gave me shelter, too."

"Oh. Really I see." Mr. Parsons looked
down to me at last, and I could see a different embarrassment replacing the first as
he met my ironic eye. "Well, Miss Er, it's aw-
fully good of you. Quite an invasion. I'm terribly sorry to be such a nuisance."

"Think nothing of it. Where are you camping, Mr. Er?"

For a moment I thought I had gone too
far. In the grey eyes regarding me through
the steam of the coffee I saw a spark that

might have been amusement. It might equally well have been annoyance—John Parsons the macho male being quietly baited by the nonentity by the fireside.

Then it was gone and he answered mildly: "On the machair. But with the wind this way it's next to impossible." Back to Ewen. "You lost your tent, too?"

"Not a tent. I've a boat. I tied up in a cove west of here, just beyond the headland."

I asked: "Can you really see the lights of this cottage from the machair?"

A perceptible pause, as Mr. Parsons turned and set his mug down on the mantelpiece. "I doubt it. But when I saw it tonight I had just struggled as far as the road. Why?"

"I just wondered."

"Whereabouts on the machair?" asked Ewen. "Pretty exposed for camping, I would have thought. Or were you near the House?"

"Which house?"

"The locals—we—call it the Big House. Or just the House. The one opposite the island where the broch is."

"Oh, yes, of course. I remember. Isn't that the Hamilton house?"

"That is right. Old Mrs. Hamilton who

lived there died recently, so the place is empty now. You know it, then? You've been to Moila before?"

"Yes, a long time ago, when I was a student."

"I wondered . . ." Ewen Mackay had been staring hard at the other man while they talked. Now he asked: "Perhaps we met then? I've been wondering if I knew you."

"Perhaps. I don't think so."

"So what brings you back here now?"

"I'm a geologist." Mr. Parsons sipped his drink placidly. He had accepted the addition from Ewen's flask. "There was something I remembered that I wanted to look at, and I thought it would be an interesting place to spend my leave. I've been working in Sydney. I'm planning to move across soon to the broch isle. There's an igneous intrusion there, with fragments of garnet peridotite— that's a rock from below the earth's crust— and I'd like to spend a bit of time there, though the rocks at the north-west end look pretty difficult to get at. But that won't interest you. . . ." The conversation had long ceased to interest me. I was feeling the need to get back to bed and to sleep. From where

I sat I could not see the clock on the mantelpiece. I got up to look, and something else caught my eye. Tucked behind the clock was a small sheaf of papers, old letters and bills, perhaps, pushed there and forgotten, presumably by the last tenants. An address was printed, and clear:

J. R. Parsons, Esq.,
at Otters' Bay,
Isle of Moila, Argyll

So "John Parsons" was perhaps not genuine all the way? When Ewen Mackay suggested that they had met before, I had thought that the other man had countered with a faintly wary look. And Ewen himself, for all his outgoing charm, had certainly acted in a way that gave pause for thought. All else apart, I could not forget that movement of his hand to his pocket when "Parsons" knocked at the door.

I carried my empty mug out to the sink, then stood in the doorway and regarded them. Neither of them had taken the slightest notice of my movements, except that Mr. Parsons was already in my empty chair and the two of them, with Ewen Mackay's

flask of whisky now standing between them,
were talking about salmon-fishing. A subject
which, I thought drily, afforded a good deal
of scope for liars.

The next move was mine. Ewen Mackay
had said he could sleep on his boat, but he
had made no move to invite Parsons to
share it with him. There might not be space
for two, and I could hardly turn the other
man out now. Safety in numbers. Let them
both stay. I may be a dish, but I am also a
don, and not prone to see emergencies
where none exist.

I said: "It's after three o'clock. I'm going
to bed. The bedroom upstairs is all ready
for my brother, and I'd prefer to have that
floor to myself anyway. I see you've sal-
vaged your sleeping-bag, Mr. Parsons. I'll
throw some towels down, and a couple of
blankets, and you can toss for it who sleeps
on the sofa and who gets the floor." I added,
out of pure malice, to Ewen: "And of course
you remember where the old loo is. Not
more than twenty yards from the back door.
Good night. Sleep well."

CHAPTER 7

The morning was calm and bright, with sunlight gilding the whins and sending a glitter across the bay. The sea still echoed the storm, foot-high waves breaking with a long *hush* against the shingle, but the sky was blue and clear. There was no sound from downstairs. I slid out of bed, put on my dressing-gown and padded out to the tiny landing. Still nothing. Downstairs there was silence, the unmistakable silence of emptiness.

I went down to make sure. Yes, they had both gone. The blankets and towels lay neatly folded on the sofa. In the scullery I found a note propped against a milk-carton on the draining-board.

It ran: "Many thanks for the hospitality.

Hope you slept well. Gone early to hunt for tent, etc. See you around, perhaps?"

It was unsigned. The reference to the tent meant either that "John Parsons" had written it, and was hoping to see me around, or that they had teamed up on a declared truce. Whatever the case, my social life on Moila seemed to have begun.

I put a cautious hand to the kettle. It was warm. So they had managed some sort of breakfast, and without waking me. More thoughtful than either of them had seemed last night. It must have been a truce. I put the kettle on again for myself, and went upstairs to dress.

I dutifully spent the morning in outer space. Once Crispin arrived, I would want to be out and about with him, so I worked till lunch-time, and was rewarded by reaching the halfway mark, and with a new idea to carry me through the next section of the story. I wrote up the notes, made myself some scrambled eggs, then decided to walk over to the post office to see if my brother had telephoned last night with any message.

Mrs. McDougall, busy behind the counter

with customers, merely shook her head at me, and signed towards the rear door of the shop, which led through into her house, where the telephone was. I went cheerfully through.

My sister-in-law answered, so quickly that she must have been right beside the telephone. She spoke almost before the first ring had finished.

"Yes? Is that the hospital?"

"No," I said, "it's Rose. Don't tell me something's turned up at this stage to stop Cris getting away?"

"Oh, Rose . . ." Nothing abrasive now about Ruth's voice. I heard her draw in a quick breath and swallow, and felt my hand tighten on the receiver as I said, more sharply than I intended:

"Please. Tell me. What's happened? Is Crispin all right?"

"Yes, he's all right. At least, he's hurt, but not badly. It's his leg—the ankle. They thought it was broken, then they said it was just a bad sprain, but apparently they want to do another X ray, so I simply don't know what's happening. He tried to phone you last night, the number you gave him, but there was something wrong with the line—"

"We had a rough night. Ruth, please, how was he hurt? What has happened?"

"He was in that train, the one that crashed last night, the derailment south of Kendal. He was on it, the sleeper for Glasgow. I thought you'd have heard about the accident. Didn't you get it on the radio?"

"No radio. Go on. About Crispin."

"He's all right, really. He phoned me himself. It wasn't a bad accident. There was a coach dragged off the line, but it didn't overturn, apparently, till everyone had been got out. Nobody killed, but a few people hurt. Cris tried to help, of course, but as soon as the ambulances came they sent him off to the local hospital, and that's where he is now. I did wonder why you hadn't called sooner—"

"Yes, well . . . Have you got the Kendal number handy?"

"Yes, but he's leaving there today. I told you they want to do another X ray, and they're sending him to Carlisle for that, the Cumberland Infirmary."

"To Carlisle? But you said he wasn't much hurt."

"No, he's not, don't worry. He sounded quite normal when he phoned, just annoyed about the holiday. He said he'd call again as soon as he heard the result of the new X ray, but not to worry about it, it's just the extra fuss they make when there's a doctor involved. You know how it is. So we'll just have to wait and see. He won't be able to do much walking, of course, but he still wants to come."

She finished on such a note of surprise that in spite of myself I laughed. "He sounds all right, anyway. Try not to worry, Ruth. I'll ring off now in case he's trying to get through to you. But I'll come up here to the post office this evening, and call you again."

"Fine. I'll get his number for you and you can call him yourself. What about you, though, Rose? Are you all right there, on your own? I don't see how he can make it before Monday, and that'll be a whole week."

I was surprised, and touched. "I'll be fine, thank you. The cottage is rather cozy, and I'm busy on a new story, so I'll have plenty to do even if the weather's bad. And when it's fine, well, it's a lovely little island, and I can have some bird-walks of my own. Give Crispin my love, Ruth, and I'll ring tonight and see how things are."

"I'll tell him. Goodbye, Rose."

"Goodbye."

Mrs. McDougall was still busy when I
went back into the shop. I collected what I
needed, and when I got to the counter I
found that she and her neighbours were dis-
cussing the train accident. Mrs. McDougall,
with a quick, concerned look at me, took
my basket from me and dumped it on the
counter.

"I hope it was not bad news, Miss
Fenemore? Did you not think that your
brother might be coming north soon? And
from London, so it would be on the line
where they had the accident, would it not?"

"Yes. And he was on that train, I'm afraid.
No, no, thank you very much, it's all right,
he isn't badly hurt, a sprained ankle, and
they say it isn't serious, but it does mean
he can't come north yet. . . ."

They exclaimed and condoled, with—
once I had assured them that nothing serious had happened to my brother—a rather
charming mixture of sympathy for me and
pleasure in the excitement of the news. I
gave them their full due, repeating all that
my sister-in-law had said, and told them that
I would hear from my brother himself that

evening, then paid for my groceries and made my escape.

I was half way home before I realized that, with all the worry and talk about the accident, I had forgotten to ask Mrs. McDougall about Ewen Mackay. Or, indeed, about John Parsons.

Not that it mattered, as I would probably not see either of them again, but the scene last night had been strange, and my curiosity was aroused.

Take Parsons first. He was, I was sure, an impostor. I refused to believe that he chanced to have the same name as the previous tenants of the cottage—unless he himself was the previous tenant, and had for some reason returned to Moila without wanting to be known? I remembered that, according to Archie McLaren, the family had used a boat, and done all their shopping in Tobermory, avoiding the islanders. An echo of Parsons' geological jargon last night sounded in my head. I had heard the word "garnets." Perhaps he really was a geologist. Perhaps he had discovered a seam— did you have a seam of garnets?—and had come back secretly to exploit it, and . . .

This was Hugh Templar taking over. Nonsense. Forget fantasy and look at fact. Take Parsons again. He had—possibly—lied about his name. He had certainly lied about seeing the cottage light. If he had been chasing his flying tent up from the machair on the west of the island, he might have got up as far as the bogland near the lochan, but surely the light from my cottage would not be visible until he had followed the road downhill past the curve and almost into Otters' Bay. Hence, his excuse for coming to the cottage was also a fake.

Now take Ewen Mackay. Maybe he had not lied, and in any case what he had said about the cottage being his home could easily be checked. He had known where the coal was kept, and the Calor gas poker, and he had had a key—which, now that I thought about it, I should certainly have asked him to hand over to me . . . But there was that unmistakable and disquieting reaction to the knocking on the door, and then the pointless deception which followed; pointless, because he must have known he could not get away with it. Had it merely been a quick try at getting rid of the intruder? But why? Then there was the rather sharp bout of questioning, which had had, on both sides, a sort of wariness about it.

And finally, the note this morning, with its suggestion of a truce between the two men.

I stopped in mid-stride, so suddenly that an oyster-catcher, which had been guddling among the reeds at the edge of the lochan, took off seawards with a screamed complaint.

Supposing, just supposing, that Mackay and Parsons had arranged to meet at the cottage. The storm had been fortuitous, an extra. Mackay, key in hand (where had he really got it from?) had made his way to Otters' Bay, and had walked straight in, assuming the cottage to be empty. I found it hard to believe that, even if he had been out of the country, his family could have moved away without his knowing. Unless, of course, they had not wanted him to know, and had seen to it that he had no address for them.

Which would say certain things about Ewen Mackay.

So, for some reason impossible to guess at, he and Parsons had arranged to meet. It was I, the unexpected tenant of the empty cottage, who was the joker in the pack. I

had made them welcome, accepted their
nonsensical stories because it didn't matter
one way or the other, and then gone oblig-
ingly off to bed and left them to their meeting. . . .

Something moved on the farther side of
the lochan, something bulky and dirty white,
caught in the bog myrtle, where it shifted
and billowed in the breeze. John Parsons'
tent? Could there have been that much truth
in what he had said?

I put the carrier with my groceries down
beside the road, and set off across the moor.
Not that it mattered (I told myself again) one
way or the other, but now that my brother's
arrival was postponed at least until Monday,
it would be good to have something of the
story checked. And of course, if the object
did happen to be the flyaway tent, its owner
would need it back.

It was not a tent, nor indeed any sort of
camping equipment. It was an old plastic
sack, probably used by a farmer and left
outside to blow away. And it could have
blown a good distance in last night's gale.
I regarded it with distaste, decided that the
rain would have washed it reasonably clean,
then dragged it clear of the bog myrtle and

looked around me for somewhere to dump it out of sight.

A fox's earth, long abandoned, and not taken over by birds or rabbits, provided the dumping-ground. I stuffed the sack down out of sight, and straightened, to see that my search had brought me above a cleft in the moorland through which a glimpse of the western machair could be seen.

It was a lovely stretch of shore, white sand and sheep-grazed turf backed by a stretch of flat, flowery meadowland. Even from where I stood I could see the white and yellow of dog-daisies and hawkear blowing in the sea-breeze like coloured veils over the green.

No sign of a tent, but over to the left, just showing, was a clump of trees thickly planted and apparently sheltered from the worst of the weather, and, standing up from among them, the chimneys of a house.

The Hamilton house, presumably. Taigh na Tuir. A big house, with no smoke rising from the chimneys. And—I walked another few yards and craned my neck to see—no sign of life in the little bay beyond, with its boat-house and jetty.

Across from the bay, beyond a narrow

stretch of water, was a small island, an islet, rather. It was long and low, humped at the northern end and tapering to the south into flat rocks washed by the sea. Just below the hump I could make out—I have good eyes—the dark outline of what must be the ruined broch, and beside that, in its shelter, was a speck of bright, alien orange. A tent. He had found his tent and had already moved to the broch island.

The oyster-catcher had come back, and was wheeling noisily over the lochan. "So what?" I said to it. So what indeed. Whatever the facts, both men had gone about their affairs, and would presumably not trouble me again. Forget it; get back to something more reasonable in the way of fantasy fiction. Another chapter today would see me nicely into the second half of my story, and this evening I would talk to Crispin and get things sorted out with him. And to-night . . . Well, I had noticed that on both front and back doors of the cottage there were stout and serviceable bolts.

As I squelched my way back round the lochan's edge towards the road, I saw the diver. Unmistakable, even though I had never seen one before; a big bird, brown and grey with a red throat, low in the water, where the wind-rippled surface managed to camouflage it in the most extraordinary way. When I had passed the lochan earlier, there had been no sign of it. It must be nesting, and now my near approach had driven it off the nest.

The thought had hardly occurred to me before the diver, with a weird-sounding cry, left the water in a noisy takeoff, and flew seawards in alarm. And there, two paces in front of my feet, was the nest.

Two huge eggs, greenish brown like the sedge, with a matt surface mottled like moss, lay in a shallow depression on the very edge of the loch, with a distinct sloping runway leading to the water, so that when alarmed the bird could slide invisibly off the eggs into a deep dive, to surface many yards away from its well-camouflaged home.

I glanced around me, quickly No one in sight; of course there wasn't. No one to see my interest in this spot on the lochan's edge. I stooped quickly and laid the back of a gentle finger against one of the eggs. It was warm. She must just have got off, and she was probably watching me from somewhere

high above the distant sea. I turned my back
on the lochan and walked a dozen paces
away from the edge before heading back
towards the road.

A sound from overhead made me look up.
The diver went over, high. I reached the
road, picked up my groceries, and left her
in peace.

I did not see Mrs. McDougall that evening. There was a girl in charge of the place,
a child of perhaps twelve, who told me that
her name was Morag, and that her auntie
had stepped out on a visit, but had said the
young lady from Camus na Dobhrain might
be there to use the telephone, and please
to go through.

For what it was worth I asked her if she
knew of a Ewen Mackay who might once
have lived at Otters' Bay, but she shook her
head.

"No." She spoke with an accent so soft
that it sounded as if an *h* was attached to
each consonant. "Not at all. There was a
Mr. and Mrs. Mackay living there, yes, but
they moved away, right to the mainland. My
auntie would know. Alastair he was called,

though, Alastair Mackay, that was gardener to old Mrs. Hamilton at the big house."

"Did they have any children?"

She hesitated, then nodded, but doubtfully. There had been—yes, she was sure there had been a boy, a long time ago, that would be. She had heard tell of him, but it was when she was very small, and she did not remember him. He would be a grown man now. She did not remember his name. Ewen? It might have been Ewen. Her auntie would know. . . .

I supposed that it did endorse part of Ewen Mackay's story. Not, of course, that it mattered. . . . I would ask Mrs. McDougall next time I was here.

On which fine piece of mental self-deceit I thanked Morag and went to the telephone.

I got straight through to my brother at the number Ruth gave me, of the hospital in Carlisle.

"What's this about another X ray?" I asked him. "Have you had the result? Is it really only a sprain?"

"That's all, but it was—still is—badly swollen, and they insisted, quite rightly, on sending me here to have another look taken at it. The first X ray showed what might have been a crack. But it's all clear. No crack. They've given me an elbow crutch, and I can make the journey perfectly well now, if I thought the blasted train would stay on the lines, but there's not much I could do once I got to Moila, is there, if I can't walk? What's it like?"

"I think it's lovely. The cottage is tiny, but it's got all we need, and there's just enough island to explore without transport. I'm afraid there's none of that—transport, I mean—except Archie McLaren's Land-Rover, the one that carries you from the harbour. You'd be a bit stuck. But would it matter? You'd be away from the job and the telephone, and you'd be resting. Unless—do you have to go back to a hospital with it, or anything?"

"No, no. There's nothing I can't deal with myself."

"Well, Archie has a boat, and he says he can take us out to the bird islands, and I'm sure we could get him to take you somewhere in the Land-Rover where you can fish. Of course, if it's really painful, forget it. I'll be fine, and I'm writing, and if it gets a bit un-lively I could perhaps find somewhere else—"

"No, why should you? I was only doubtful because of spoiling your holiday. I can manage perfectly well, and I'd hate to miss Moila."

"It would spoil my holiday far more if you didn't come," I said. "So risk the train, will you? And do you want me to ring the Oban hotel and tell them what's happened and change the booking? You have? That's great . . . It really is lovely here, and—well, I didn't want to overpersuade you, but I found a red-throated diver's nest today, perfectly lovely, two eggs, and I didn't bring a camera. Didn't think we'd need two, and mine's not nearly as good as yours, even if I could take half as good a picture."

"And you don't call that overpersuading? I'll be there," said my brother. "Expect me on Monday's ferry, then. If I know anything about it, I'll be well and truly mobile by then."

"Physician, heal thyself," I said, laughing, and rang off, with a lightened heart.

CHAPTER 8

Next morning was fair and sunny, with a breeze, but I journeyed duly into outer space, to tackle the problems of my party on Terra Secunda. Their difficulties were rapidly threatening to become too much for them, and consequently for me, too. In those circumstances I have always found it wise to abandon effort and leave the sub-conscious mind to sort things out while the conscious mind does something quite different. Goes for a walk, for example, and takes a look at the Hamilton house and that delectable stretch of milk-white sand bor-dering the machair.

I followed the cliff path which led steeply up out of Otters' Bay and then westward over the headland for something less than half a mile, to bring me in sight of the bay

I had seen yesterday. Just inland from this, against its background of sheltering trees, stood the house.

A high dry-stone wall enclosed the land round it for some four or five acres, and inside this enclosure were more trees, oak and fir and beech above the massed colours of rhododendrons in flower, with one big horse-chestnut in full bloom holding its creamy candelabra out across the wall. A stone archway in the seaward wall spanned a tall ironwork gate.

Straight across from the house lay the broch islet. Now, with the tide low, the causeway connecting the islet with Moila's mainland was high and dry, running across at the narrowest point of the channel. It consisted of natural slabs of flattish stone which at some time in the past had been leveled by wedges, and "helped" in places by concrete, to form a crossing-place. But time and tide and neglect had eaten away at the structure so that even at low tide, with the slabs fully exposed, crossing would be tricky.

To either side of this causeway was a tumble of half-exposed rocks glossy with black seaweed, where the water rose and fell, barely stirring the weed. Apart from this crossing-point the channel seemed, even at this stage of the tide, to be fairly deep. Deep enough, at any rate, for a boat to get in to the boat-house which was tucked in under the cliff at the southern end of the bay, below the path where I stood. Beside the boat-house a jetty thrust out into the water, and from this a weedy, once-gravelled path led along above the beach to the stone archway which was the garden gate of Taigh na Tuir.

I made my way down into the bay. That alone would have been worth the scramble round the cliff path. I had never seen anything like it before, a crescent of dazzling white, where a million pearly shells had been pounded and smashed by the Atlantic swells into fine sand, marked only by the tides, and above the tide-marks by the myriad criss-crossing prints of sea-birds.

It was not to be resisted. I sat down and took off my shoes and socks—I was wearing slacks and trainers—and then walked across the bay, luxuriating in the feel of the fine warm sand under my bare feet. I went right down to the sea's edge, but the water was too cold for pleasure, so I retreated to

the dry level and sat down to brush the sand
off my feet and put on my shoes again.

This done, I stood for a moment looking
across at the broch islet. Directly across the
channel was another, bigger bay, a long
curving stretch of lovely white sand, with
above it a sweep of green turf and bracken
rising as far as the dark circle of the broch.
The whole place was alive with the wings
and calls of sea-birds. It was very tempting,
but it would be stupid to go across now,
until I knew more about the tides. I wondered where John Parsons was; looking for
his garnet-studded "intrusion," whatever
that was, on the other side of the island? I
could see the tent from here, pitched in a
hollow not far from the broch wall. The en-
trance flaps were shut.

I trod up through the seaweed at the edge
of the beach, then followed the path to the
gate in the garden wall. I peered through the
bars. Inside the grounds the path continued,
curving up between the overgrown rhododendrons in the direction of the house. I
hesitated. There would presumably be a
driveway of sorts leading from the back of
the house to the road and my easiest way
home. To try and get to it by going round

outside the garden wall meant plowing through waist-high nettles and clumps of bramble. So . . . ? So I opened the gate and went through.

There had never been much of a garden, only the rhododendrons flowering red and pink and lilac, where bees droned happily. Beyond the wild tangle of flowers I could just see the upper story of the house, grey stone with tall sashed windows and a roof of grey slate with its unsmoking chimney stacks. There were curtains in the windows. The place must still be furnished, then. I tried to remember when Mrs. McDougall had said the old lady had died. February? And Archie McLaren had told me that the house would probably be sold, so it was to be supposed that at any time now people might be coming to look at it.

It was the subconscious mind taking over again. I found myself half way up the path between the rhododendrons before the conscious mind caught up with the fact that, though there had been a padlock on the garden gate, the gate had been unlocked. So, surely there could be no objection to someone taking a look at a place that would soon be up for sale anyway? I crossed a lawn

that badly needed cutting, and started on a
cautious tour of the Hamilton house.

I doubt if there are many normal women
who can resist looking at houses. I believe,
in fact, that when a house is up for sale more
than half the people who look over it are not
prospective buyers, but merely ladies who
cannot resist exploring someone else's
house. I had never done that, but I was not
immune. I trod carefully up to the most im-
portant-looking window, and peered in.

The drawing-room. A rather lovely fireplace, with a hideous overmantel. Faded
carpet and curtains. Typical family paintings
of dim-looking not-quite-Raeburns, and im-
probable horses and dogs. Round tables
with skirts, their surfaces smothered with
photographs. Sagging armchairs with faded
covers, not too clean. A quite awful vase in
one corner, full of dried pampas grass.

The dining-room. More portraits, if possible duller still, and lightened by a couple of
horrendous still-lifes, dead hares and poul-
try, staring eyes and blood congealing from
beaks and nostrils; just the thing to give one
an appetite for meals.

The gun-room . . . But enough of that. It
was a very ordinary, rather pleasant, High-

land country house; originally a shooting-lodge and of no great size or importance for the day when it was built. And meant only for summer and early autumn; no heating apparatus except the open fires, and a kitchen rather on a par for mod cons with my cottage at Otters' Bay.

The only thing that was quite extraordinary was what I found when I got as far as the back premises.

The back door was standing open.

My excuse, a thin one, is still the subconscious mind. I did knock at the door, then, when there was no response, took a couple of steps through into a passage floored with stone slabs and containing nothing but some buckets of coal and a rack of ancient clothes, gardening clobber by the look of it. In spite of the open door, the place smelled of damp and disuse.

The kitchen door was on my right. I pushed it open. Emptiness again; somehow a kitchen, which is the warm heart of any house, is the worst place of all when it is disused. The house is dead without the warmth and the smells of cooking and the pulse of daily living. In the stuffy silence the

sound of the cold tap slowly dripping was
almost cozy; a substitute heartbeat. Even
so, my presence felt like an intrusion. But
as I turned to go something caught my attention. A key-rack just beside the doorway,
with keys hanging there, labelled. One hook
was empty; the hook labelled "C. na Dobhrain." Otters' Bay.

For no good reason, that settled it, by
which I mean that what conscience I had
was put to sleep by sheer, raging curiosity.
Could my night-time visitor have called in
here to pick up the key he had showed me,
and left the back door open at the same
time? Had he put into this bay first, then
come up past the house and, finding it open,
taken the key? But why should he trouble?
If he had really only been looking for shelter
and a place to doss down for the night, why
look further than this? Why make the wet
and stormy trek to Otters' Bay? Even if he
had thought his parents were still there—
which I found hard to believe—he could
have visited them in the morning.

Somehow, this seemed to justify what I
had done. If there was indeed any mystery
about Ewen Mackay's visit to my cottage,
the clue to it might well be here, in the house

he had claimed to be familiar with. More, he had hinted, unless I had misread him, at a connection with the family. Perhaps he even considered himself to have some kind of claim to the place? At least, then, the note that had been left for me ("See you around?") gave me some excuse for trespassing now.

I went on down the passage, towards the green baize door that closed the back premises off from the gentry's quarters, pushed the door open, and trod tentatively into the front hall.

This was darkish, lighted only by the stained-glass fan-window over the shut front door. To one side stood a heavy oak table piled with the usual clutter—magazines, newspapers, a couple of heavy electric torches, some anonymous boxes. Opposite this another, smaller table held gloves, a sou'wester, and a gardening basket crammed with implements. There was a brass stand holding walking sticks, and a dark oak settle where someone had thrown down a Barbour coat and an old anorak. Some pairs of boots and wellingtons were lined up beside it, and on the wall, above a crude oil landscape that seemed meant to depict the moor where the diver nested, was

a long rack presumably meant for fishing-
rods.

The impression of a house where the oc-
cupants had just walked out for a stroll in
the garden was very strong. My presence
there seemed, suddenly, an intrusion, my
curiosity, if not an outrage, at any rate no
excuse for going any further.

I turned to go out the way I had come.
But even as I turned, I heard something. A
sound from upstairs. The creak of a door.

My heart gave a jump, then resumed
something like its normal beat as I registered the fact that even in an empty house
there were drafts, and doors moved and
creaked with no one to push them. But I did
make for the baize door a little more quickly
than on my way in, and in the semi-darkness
stumbled over one of the wellingtons, kick-
ing it half way across the floor. I only saved
myself from falling by clutching at the arm
of the oak settle.

Something came down the stairs like an
avalanche. A pair of powerful arms seized
me from behind, jerking me upright and off
my feet. Clutched tightly to the breast of a
Shetland sweater I took breath and
screamed.

The arms, suddenly nerveless, dropped me, and the Shetland sweater retreated smartly. I fell onto the settle, hit my elbow on the carved armrest, and drew in my breath to scream again.

"Don't!" said John Parsons hastily. "Please don't! I'm terribly sorry. I thought it was—I didn't realize it was a girl. I wouldn't dream of— Oh, it's you."

I abandoned the scream. I rubbed my elbow, regarding him thoughtfully. He towered over me, looking anxious, rather flustered, and not in the least dangerous. I said: "Well, who says it first?"

"Says what?"

" 'What are you doing here?' So what *are* you doing here? I know you found your tent, but perhaps you thought this might be a more comfortable bivouac than my cottage? Is that it?"

"Not quite. I—actually, the tent was never lost, but—"

"Where's Ewen Mackay? Is he sleeping here, too?"

"No. Why should he be? Then he isn't with you?"

"No, he is not." Because I felt both guilty and embarrassed, I reacted sharply. "For goodness' sake, surely you didn't fall for all that nonsense of his the other night? I'd never seen him before in my life! I think he must have taken the key for my cottage from the board by the kitchen there. It seems to be true that the cottage used to be his home, but you don't carry a big old-fashioned key like that around in your pocket for years, so I don't see how else he got it. If he broke in—but then why come to the cottage at all? And why should you? Did you break in here, too, or has the back door been unlocked the whole time?"

He answered only one question out of this barrage, and it was enough. "Neither," he said. "I had a key."

"You had a key?" The repetition sounded stupid. But the situation was itself a repetition of Wednesday night's adventure. "You, too?" I took a breath. "But perhaps—did you have an appointment to look over the house, or something?"

"Not quite. The house is mine."

"Oh, no! Not again!" I must have sounded, if possible, more stupid than ever. "Yours?"

He smiled suddenly "Yes, mine. I'm not sure how long wills take to prove, but I was

Aunt Emily's only living relative, and it's always been understood that the place would come to me. In any case, someone had to come and try to sort things out. I'm Neil Hamilton."

I managed to stop myself from repeating that, too. "I see. Well, thank you for telling me, Mr. Parsons.

He said, apologetically: "I'm sorry about that, but there were reasons. Why don't we go somewhere more comfortable and discuss them? I do owe you that. In here?"

He opened the drawing-room door and ushered me through.

CHAPTER 9

He crossed to the french window and pushed it open. Seen in this light, and in the light of what he had now told me, I studied him afresh.

He was tall, and looked sunburned, as if he had spent time recently in a climate far from the Hebrides. Not handsome, but nice-looking in a way I had usually rather depre-cated, if not despised: not the lean and craggy looks that I had always admired, but a blunt-featured face with a wide mouth, dark eyes tilted slightly down at the outer corners, and an untidy thatch of brown hair of which a couple of locks fell over a broad forehead, and were from time to time irrita-bly brushed back. I saw that he was, in his turn, studying me. He would be seeing, I thought, an unremarkable young woman, rather too solemn, with thought-lines developing too fast between level dark brows; dark brown hair and grey eyes; tolerable nose and mouth, and—my only real claims to beauty—a good figure and a fine, fair skin.

"So I take it that you're just here for a holiday, on your own, Miss Fenemore? Or do you prefer Ms.?"

"Sorry?"

"Do you prefer Ms.? If that is how one says it?"

"It sounds just like a goose hissing. Unpronounceable—and unnecessary, unless you don't want people to know you're not married. Which I'm not, but I still hate it."

"You sound a bit fierce. I wasn't sure. Some ladies insist."

"Not this one. Actually, if you could say it was short for 'Mistress,' which is rather nice, and very correct in Scotland . . . I'd certainly settle for that. Or, well, 'Rose' would be the easiest, wouldn't it? Sorry, don't tell me, I know. I'm being priggish. But I like words, and that's a non-word if ever there was one."

"Well, it's a good hobby-horse."

"Hobby-horse nothing. It's my job. I teach

English at Cambridge. Haworth College. And yes, this is just a holiday. My brother was to have come with me; he's a doctor working in Petersfield, and he's a dedicated bird-watcher and photographer. He was to have joined me this week, but his train met with an accident, so he's been detained for a few days with an injured ankle. He's coming over as soon as he can. Monday, I hope. That's all about me. Your turn, Mr. Hamilton-Parsons."

"Oh, well. The Parsons bit was a not very inspired lie. You saw it, didn't you, when you got up to go upstairs? The postcard on the mantelpiece?"

"Yes. But the point is, why?"

"I couldn't give my own name, till I found out what that fellow was up to. I should have thought up something better on the way over, but no one could think in that wind. It was all I could do to keep my feet."

"So you knew he was 'up to' something? You mean you knew from the start that he had no connection with me?"

"No, no. I did take you for a couple staying there together, and normally I would have retreated smartly and come back here again, but for what had already happened.

Look, why don't you sit down and make
yourself comfortable? I'd better start at the
beginning, and it's a long story."

I did as he suggested. He stayed on his
feet by the window.

"I'm Neil Hamilton, as I told you, and Mrs.
Hamilton was my great-aunt. I'm a geologist—that bit was true—and until recently
I've been working in Sydney. Then I heard
about Aunt Emily's death. The end came
rather suddenly, so I couldn't have got back
in time to see her, but I flew over as soon
as I was free, to see what had to be done.
There's no one else. I was very fond of her
when I was a child, and used to spend most
of my holidays up here with her—my father
was in the Consular Service, so my parents
spent a lot of their time abroad. But latterly
I've been here very little; in fact it must be
at least fifteen years since I stayed here for
any length of time. . . . Yes, I had my four-
teenth birthday here. Uncle Fergus gave me
a gun, I remember. He still had hopes of me,
but I'm afraid I never enjoyed killing things.
Still don't." He smiled. "He'd have been
ashamed of me. Not the ideal Scottish laird
at all."

As he spoke, he had been wandering

round the room, picking up photographs, looking at books, standing in front of the pictures; a sort of half-abstracted and apparently unemotional tour down Memory Lane. I brought him back to the matter in hand.

"And what brought you to my cottage in the middle of the night, with that story about your tent blowing away? In fact, why a tent at all? All those lies for Ewen Mackay before you'd even met him?"

He turned back to me. "Yes, we come to that. They were lies, but as it happens I had met him before. Many years ago, when we were boys. If you remember, he half recognized me. I had already recognized him, but fifteen years or so, boy to man, is a big change, and I doubt if he got it. In fact I'm sure he didn't. We talked late that night, and he would surely have said something."

"I see. Or rather, I don't, yet. Are you telling me that because you recognized him you had to put on that charade? That you had some reason to distrust him?"

He nodded. "As a boy he was—well, shall we just say undependable? But it wasn't that. I had my lies ready before I ever recognized him. I'd seen him earlier that night, here at the house, behaving in a way that made me very anxious to find out what he was doing here on Moila."

"Here? You were here then? Everyone said the place was empty."

"It was. I'd just arrived, and I hadn't been up to the village yet, or seen anyone. Still haven't, if it comes to that."

"How did you get here?"

"I have a boat. Hired. Aunt Emily sold the one that was here; she had no use for it latterly. I came across from Oban—made a run for it, with the weather worsening all the time, but got here safely and made straight for our bay. Put the boat into the boat-house and made the doors fast, then came up to the house. I'd been to see my great-aunt's solicitors in Glasgow and they gave me the keys. I'd bought all I needed in Oban, so I just came up here and got myself settled in. It was pretty late and I was tired, so I found my old room and went straight to bed. It was well after midnight, getting on for one o'clock, when I went to open the bedroom window, and saw someone coming through the garden from the bay."

He stopped prowling at last, and dropped into one of the easy chairs facing me.

"Of course at first I just thought it was someone from a boat that had been driven in by the weather. You remember that night was pretty dark, so I couldn't have seen if there was a boat tied up at the jetty. The chap had a torch. Coming to ask for shelter, I thought, though why he couldn't sleep in his boat . . . As I said, it's quiet down there in the channel even in a storm. That made me wonder what he wanted, so I stood and watched. He got as far as the lawn, just out there, and then he stopped and stood, seemingly just staring at the house. That seemed odd, too, in all that rain. Anyway, I came downstairs. The front door was still locked and bolted—I'd only used the back one since I'd got here—and the keys were out the back, so I came in here to open these french windows. I didn't put any lights on, and when I got into this room I was thankful I hadn't. I found him trying the window."

"Well," I said reasonably, "in that storm, and if he thought the house was empty—"

"I know. I thought so, too. But he didn't just try the handle. He had some kind of tool, and he was trying to lever the window open. I stood there like a fool, watching him.

Somehow one isn't prepared for that kind
of situation. . . . Then I thought, well, I'll
have to tackle him somehow, so the best
way, rain or no rain, was to go out the back
way and take him from behind."

"He had a gun," I said.

That startled him. "Had he indeed?"

"I think so. But go on, please!"

"I'm not exactly a man of action—that
kind of action. Who is, except in television
series? There used to be guns in the house,
of course, but it never occurred to me to
look if they were still there. But I must have
felt the need for some support, because I
found I'd grabbed hold of one of my ham-
mers—a geologist is always armed with a
hammer—and when I got through to the
back of the house he was there already, at
the kitchen window."

"Good heavens! So?"

"I'm not quite sure what might have happened then, but for some reason he gave
up. He could have forced the window in
time, anyone could, but he seemed suddenly to think better of it. One moment he
was there on the sill, and then suddenly he
was gone. I ran upstairs to see what I
could, and there he was, torch and all, run-

ning down the garden and then dodging his way up to the cliff path, and fast, as if he knew exactly where he was going. Of course I knew the path led to the Camus na Dobhrain, and the lawyers had told me that the cottage was let to a girl, so I wondered why he was headed there. I mean, there was nowhere else he could have been going. So I decided to follow along and see what was going on."

"But you had a duffel bag. . . . Was that just scene-painting to go with your story about the tent?"

"More or less. I have got a tent here, as it happens, because I want to work on Eilean na Roin—that's Seal Island, where the broch is—and the tides are awkward, so I need a base there. I took the tent across next morning."

"I know. I saw it. But surely you weren't really here as a student? If you'd met Ewen Mackay then—"

"He'd have recognized me now, of course. Yes, that was a lie, too. Not the igneous intrusion—that's there all right; a colleague of mine told me about it—and I did intend to work there while I was here in

Moila. Something to do while the estate
business is being settled."

"And did you bring the hammer, too,
when you came chasing over to my cottage?"

"Er—I hardly remember. I don't suppose
I did. And then, of course, when he opened
the door to me, I recognized him. And since
he obviously hadn't recognized me, I didn't
want to connect myself with the house, until
I'd found out what his game was."

"And mine?"

"Well, yes. And yours."

I smiled. "Fair enough. But whatever your
motives for coming over, I'm glad you did.
If he was really up to no good the situation
might have turned awkward—though as it
happens he was perfectly civil, and I wasn't
nervous."

"I could see that. And that made me wonder if you were in it, too, and he'd had a
rendezvous at the cottage. I found out next
morning that his boat was in Halfway House,
but when I first saw him I had no idea he
was a Moila man, and it didn't occur to me
that he would know the mooring there. I just
assumed he was making for Otters' Bay." A
pause, while he seemed to be studying the

pattern of the carpet. Then he looked up at me. "What reason did he give you for coming all the way over to Otters' Bay when he could perfectly well have slept in his boat?"

"Oh, that the cottage had been his home, and he said—or pretended—that he didn't know his people had moved away. I'm sure it was true that he didn't know the place was let to me."

He was silent for a while, frowning at the prospect, from the window, of the neglected garden. "Well, I still can't imagine what his game is, and I can't say that I like it."

"When the pair of you went off to find your tent, what happened?"

"Nothing much. We made a token search for it on the way back to the bay, but then he went straight to his boat, and it's gone, and I've no idea where to. No sign of him anywhere near you since then?"

"None. So what happens now?"

"Nothing, let's hope. I honestly don't see what's to be done except wait and keep our eyes open. Nothing's happened to justify reporting to the police. The man did nothing, after all, except shoot a line to you, and if it's a crime to wander round an empty house

on a wild night, trying the windows,
well . . ."

"I take your point. Nobody's going to listen. Just one other detail; the key of my cottage. I don't believe he's been carrying a
huge old-fashioned thing like that around
ever since he left. I see there's a place on
your key-board by the back door for the cottage key, and it's missing. Unless you took
it?" He shook his head. "Then if Ewen
Mackay took it, that wasn't his first visit to
this house. He'd been here before, and—"

"And left the french windows open so that
he could get in again! You're right! I did find
the window open, and locked it myself because of the way it was rattling in the wind.
I thought nothing of it, just that whoever
closed the house up had overlooked it. So
that could be it. He came back, and when
he found the place locked up again, he got
a scare, or he just decided to play it safe,
and made off."

"He did tell me he'd been to the house,"
I said. "He made out that he'd gone to take
a nostalgic look at it, and of course he never
said he'd tried to get in, or that he'd been
before. . . . I must say I thought at the time
that it was a pretty rough night to choose

for a sentimental journey. . . . He did throw out a hint—" I stopped.

"Yes? About what?"

"No. It was—well, personal. Nothing to do with this."

"Till we know what 'this' is," he said reasonably, "everything may be to do with it."

"I suppose so."

"So, go on, please. What did he hint at?"

"Honestly I doubt if it matters, and I don't want . . . Oh, all right. He hinted that he might actually be connected with your family At least that's what I thought he was trying to convey."

To my relief, he laughed. "That figures. Great-Uncle Fergus's love-child, adopted, presumably for a consideration, by the gardener? Don't worry, I've heard that one before. And a few others even wilder. He lived in a fantasy world of his own, even as a small boy He used to lie for no reason at all, as if he enjoyed it. I was only a couple of years older myself, but I knew enough never to believe a word he said. Did he shoot any more lines to you? Tell you where he's been since he left Moila?"

"Only that he'd been abroad. I gathered that he'd been around in some pretty exciting—oh, do you mean he might have made that up, too? He didn't actually sail round the Horn?"

"I'll believe that when I've seen the boat's log," said Neil drily, "and only then after it's been checked by an expert. And talking of checking, I'd better have a look through the house to see if anything's missing. The lawyers gave me an inventory. Blast. I had hoped to take my time over sorting out the house contents, but I'd better take a look straight away—at any rate for the movable stuff. Tell me, how sure were you that he had a gun?"

"Not sure at all. It was just the way his hand flew to his pocket when you hammered at the door."

"Hm. Then let's hope that was window-dressing, too. Well . . ." He set his hands to the chair arms, as if about to rise. "He's gone, so perhaps that's the end of the mystery. When did you say your brother was coming?"

"Monday, I hope."

"Then all we can do is keep our eyes open for the next couple of days, and you see that your doors are locked and bolted at night."

"I certainly will. And you?"

"As you saw, I've got my tent set up now on the island. I'll work there, but I'll come back and sleep in the house. If Ewen does come back, he'll see the tent, and if he thinks that 'Parsons' is safely out of the way, then whatever his interest is in the house, he'll no doubt show it. And I'll be here to tackle him, hammer and all."

"And I?"

"Stay safe at Otters' Bay, and wait for your brother. Forget all this," he said, with decision.

"I could try," I said.

He got to his feet then, and I followed suit. The sun, slanting in through the window, showed up the faded shabbiness of the room, but outside the treetops were golden and the bees were loud in the roses. The scents of the garden, blowing in through the open window, had removed the last trace of stuffiness from the room. It smelt fresh and warm. He moved to open the door to the hall.

"So before I see you safely home, would you like a cup of tea?"

"I'd love it. But there's not the slightest need for you to see me home."

"Probably not. But I'm going to," he said

cheerfully. His spirits seemed suddenly to have cleared. The sun, perhaps. "This way, then, Mistress Fenemore. But I forgot, you've already explored my kitchen, haven't you? After you."

CHAPTER 10

After tea we walked down through the remains of the garden. The path was ankle-deep in weeds, and to either side the overgrown rhododendrons, heavy with flowers, crowded in over the mosses and ferns of a mild damp climate. Wild honeysuckle clambered everywhere, and the air was sweet with it.

"We'll take a short cut. The grass is quite dry," said Neil, and led the way through a gap in the rhododendrons into a broad grassed walk leading directly down towards the sea. At the end was an opening, now almost closed by the crowding trees and bushes, through which one could see the glimmer of the sea and the northernmost hill of the broch islet.

I was looking at this, and not at where I

was putting my feet. I stubbed my toe,
swore, tripped, and almost fell, to be saved
by a robust grip above the elbow.

"Are you all right?" He held me while I
stood on one leg to massage the injured toe.
"It's so long since anything was done here,
the place is cluttered with storm damage. Is
it bad?"

"Not a bit. It's okay now. Thank you." He
let me go, and I massaged my arm instead,
where he had gripped me. "But you know
how a stubbed toe hurts. It must have been
a pretty hefty bit of storm damage. It felt
like—yes, look at this!"

Deep in the grass, embedded like a
sleeper in soft green, lay a naked figure. Perhaps four feet high, a girl, daintily made, her
body stained and streaked green with moss.
A marble girl, once white, blind eyes staring.
Somehow, you could see that the eyes were
blinded by tears.

"I tripped over her hand. I hope I didn't
damage it. No, it looks all right. Who is she?"

"I think she's meant to be Echo." He
stooped to push the grass and ferns back.
"She stood there, can you see where the
plinth is? And there was water in a stone
basin, but yes, that's broken, too. I remem-

ber when she arrived, and was set up. My great-uncle brought them from Italy; he was terribly proud of them." He laughed suddenly. "I'm no judge, but I believe they're quite good. Dear old Uncle Fergus's one successful venture into the art world. His taste in pictures was pretty awful. You may have noticed."

"I wouldn't have said a word, but yes, I noticed." I was still looking down at the girl in the grass. The breeze stirred the shadows over her, as if she breathed. "I'm not an expert, either, but I love Echo. You said 'them.' Are there more?"

"There were four. There should be another across from this, on the other side. Yes, here it is, and still standing."

He crossed the ride, pushing some of the strangling boughs aside, to show the other figure, which was in fact kneeling. The stone basin was intact, and half filled with black and dirty rainwater. A marble boy, a youth, knelt over the water, gazing down.

"Narcissus?"

"I suppose so," he said. "I don't remember. The others are along there, at the end of this walk. My great-uncle made a little belvedere there, with that view of the sea and the Eilean na Roin. I can't see them, though. The trees grow at such a rate here that you can hardly even see the sea."

He turned and stood looking back at the house. In this sunlight the dilapidation showed up clearly, and the mess of the garden.

There was something in his face which made me say, gently:

"But beauty vanishes, beauty passes,
However rare, rare it be."

"What's that?"

"Walter de la Mare. *And when I crumble, who shall remember/That lady of the West Country?* and heaven knows, there's beauty here and to spare, without anything men have built."

He was silent, still looking at the house. Eventually, he said, as if to himself: "I'm glad I came back." Then, briskly, to me: "I sometimes think it's a mistake to have been happy when one was a child. One should always want to go on, not back. Poor old Echo. Maybe whoever buys the house will set her up again where she can see Narcissus—and much good did that ever do the poor girl."

"Will you really sell?"

"What else can I do? I can't live here."

"I suppose as a holiday house it is a bit far from Sydney."

"Not Sydney. I was going to tell you earlier, but somehow Ewen's misdeeds threw us off track—I'll be in Cambridge next term. Living at Emmanuel."

"Well, that's great! Congratulations. You'll be looking forward to it."

"Sure. And more than ever now." He did not explain what he meant, but went on rather quickly to tell me about the appointment, and for a while we talked about Cambridge, and places and people that we both knew well. He would be living in college at first—Emmanuel was his own college—but he would like, he said, to find a place of his own, preferably outside the town.

This brought us back rather abruptly to the present, and the house he already possessed. It appeared that although Taigh na Tuir had not been formally put on the market, there had already been some interest shown. A London agent, apparently acting for someone anxious for an island property, had made a good offer "sight unseen," and Neil's solicitors (who knew the place and the difficulties involved) had strongly advised him to accept it. Neil had taken their advice, and there had been the exchange of missives which, I gathered, served in Scotland as a binding contract.

"Binding on me, that is," said Neil, "though the buyer, once he sees the property, may still withdraw."

"So there's still a chance you could keep it?"

He shook his head. "Not really. How could I? Even if I didn't have a job that keeps me at the other end of the country for most of the year, this sort of place couldn't provide a living. Originally the family owned the whole island, which holds about four farms, but those have all been sold off now, and there's no land except the stretch from Otters' Bay to the other end of the machair. And Eilean na Roin, of course." He shrugged, a gesture at once apologetic and dismissive. "But even if the estate was still intact, there's hardly a living in farming nowadays. Or so I understand. There certainly wouldn't be for me. I don't know a tup from a gimmer. Shall we go?"

When we reached the jetty we paused for a few moments to look across at the islet. Gulls were wheeling over it, and the noise was incessant. A different noise made itself heard, and there among the circling gulls, high up, a fighter plane among the domestic craft, tore a peregrine falcon.

"She nests on the mainland cliffs," said Neil. "Ever since I remember there's been a peregrine on that cliff. I tried to climb down to the nest once. I was about eleven years old. They caught me at it, luckily, before I'd gone over the edge. Over there, see? The white streaks high on the cliff." He was pointing northwards, to the cliffs towering beyond the machair. I could just make out the spot he indicated.

I said, with reverence: "My God."

He laughed. "Makes your blood run cold to think what small boys will do without a second thought."

"I don't suppose my brother will have any hope of a picture there, even from a boat and with a telephoto lens . . . But if he can manage it, may I please take him over to the island to look at the birds there? What's its name again?"

"Eilean na Roin. It means Island of the

Seals. They come ashore there to breed. Go over by all means, but do watch the tides. The crossing's only really safe for about two hours to either side of low tide. You see that rock there, shaped a bit like a shoe?" He pointed at a rock near the causeway. "When the sea gets to the base of that, the tide's already too high, and it comes in like a horse trotting, as they say. You don't need my permission to go over there anyway. Didn't you know there's no law of trespass in Scotland?"

"Not even in your house?"

He smiled. "That was a pleasure. The whole visit has been a pleasure. I'd have liked to prolong it by asking you to supper, but . . ." A gesture finished it for him: the empty house, the deserted kitchen.

"That was very nicely done," I said appreciatively. "Aren't you taking a risk, though? I mean, I'm a don. What makes you think I can cook as well as get stroppy about words?"

"The fact that you came to Moila and took that godforsaken cottage—and that your brother agreed to come with you," said Neil cheerfully. "Besides, I saw eggs and cheese and all sorts of stuff in the cupboard when

I spent the night there. Do I take it that I'm invited, Mistress Fenemore?"

"Well, of course, and for pity's sake stop reminding me about that. My name's Rose. Just tell me, though—failing our meeting this afternoon, what were you planning to do? Suck gulls' eggs?"

"Come over to Otters' Bay again and beg for shelter. What else?"

"Considering you told me that you'd taken supplies on in Oban and that you managed perfectly well all of yesterday, and that your boat is probably stiff with tins and even bottles—"

"Bottles! Now, that's a thought. We'll collect a couple here and now . . . And you might be right about the supplies. Will you dine with me tomorrow, please? And if your brother should happen to make it, bring him too, of course."

"At the house? Lights on, chimney smoking, and your lovely alibi wasted? Had you forgotten your plan, Mr. Parsons?"

"Do you know, I had. And how right you are." He sounded, suddenly, irritated. "And how absurd to think that there's any need for all this cloak and dagger stuff. . . . Yes, I'd forgotten. All right, we'll give it another day or two, but I'm seeing you back home now, and don't try to talk me out of it. I'm starving. And for pity's sake call me Neil."

"All right." It was extraordinary, but suddenly we seemed to be on quite different terms. "All right, I'll feed you. But only if you do get those bottles, and quickly. I'm starving, too."

"Red or white? And is it gin or sherry?" He was at the boat-house door, taking a key from his pocket. "No, never mind. I'll bring the lot. And I promise to help with the washing up."

CHAPTER 11

Saturday morning, and once again a fair and breezy day, so fair that I decided to give myself a holiday from writing, and go straight after breakfast to pick up the supplies I would need for the weekend. Mrs. McDougall had promised to have milk and bread for me, and there might possibly be mail, brought over by the morning's ferry.

Neil had told me to try and forget about the "mystery," and this proved surprisingly easy to do. On such a morning, with the sky full of larks, and the banks beside the road stiff with fox-gloves and wild roses, the odd events of Wednesday night seemed remote, and indeed little more than odd. So I busied myself, as I walked, with plans for supper on Monday night, when I hoped that my brother would be here, and I had invited Neil to join us.

When I drew near the village I could see two girls sitting on the parapet of the little bridge. They seemed to be watching me, and then one of them waved, and I saw that they were Megan Lloyd and Ann Tracy.

Megan's friend Ann was a complete contrast to the dark, rather intense Welsh girl. She was a land agent's daughter from somewhere in Norfolk, tall and fair, with heavy gilt hair curling down over her shoulders, and a long, slim, slightly drooping body that had a certain elegance. Her oval face, with its thick fair eyebrows, blue eyes, and high colour, and the small mouth with the slight droop there, too, looked deceptively gentle. In fact I knew her for a tough-minded young woman with feminist leanings and rather more interest in student politics than would be helpful in her academic work. At present, Ann led and Megan followed, but that would sort itself out in the long run. Ann had a good brain, but Megan had it in her to be brilliant.

When the greetings and exclamations were over, they told me that they had been staying on Mull for a few days, and had just arrived on Moila, and were putting up at the post office with Mrs. McDougall.

"She told us where your cottage was, and we've got a map. Not that you really need one on Moila. We were planning to come down today and see you." That was Ann. Megan put in quickly:

"We knew you were on your own. Mrs. McDougall told us about your brother. We're terribly sorry. Is he badly hurt?"

"No, no. He says it's nothing, and he should know. He's a doctor. I've talked with him on the telephone and with any luck he should be over here on Monday. I don't know how well he'll be able to get about, but we'll manage somehow. I'd love you to see the cottage. Were you thinking of visiting me this morning?"

"Yes," said Ann, "but then Mrs. McDougall said you'd be coming up here for your shopping, so we waited."

"And don't worry," said Megan, patting a haversack that lay beside her on the parapet. "We've got masses of food for a picnic, so you don't have to feed us. We were going to say hullo to you, and then walk round to that little island—it's called Seal Island—I can't say the Gaelic name but Mrs. McDou-

gall told me that's what it means. It's the
one with the broch on it. It looks as if there's
a path over from your cottage, so perhaps
we could walk round there and then come
back to you for tea?"

"Well, of course you may, but did you ask
about the tides? That's not a bridge that's
marked on the map, it's a causeway that's
covered most of the time. I was down there
yesterday, and I doubt if you'll be able to
cross much before two o'clock. Why not
make sure? I think I saw tide tables in the
post office."

While the girls studied the tide tables I
bought my groceries. There were no letters,
and to my relief no messages either. No
news being good news, that meant Crispin
on Monday. I told Morag (Mrs. McDougall
was busy over the tide tables with Ann and
Megan), then went out to wait for them.

It appeared that my guess about the tide
had been near enough.

"Low tide at four-oh-four," said Ann, "and
we've been warned to leave not one second
later than six, or be marooned all night. Oh
well, we'll just have to have our picnic on
the mainland. Did you say you were down
there yesterday, Dr. Fenemore? What's it

like? There's a house marked, right beside the bridge—the causeway, I mean—so will there be people about?"

"The house is empty, and the place is quite lovely. I was just too late yesterday to go across, but the islet looked marvelous. There's quite a lot of the broch showing, too, almost the complete circle, with one very high bit where I'm told there are steps going up to what's left of the top level, with a view."

"It sounds terrific," said Megan.

Ann made a face. "You can have it." Then, to me: "We went to Orkney last summer, and she made me crawl in through a ghastly tunnel into some underground charnel-house. Never again! It's bad enough now, but it must have been really something when it was occupied. Apparently they ate nothing but shellfish, and just dropped the shells on the floor when they'd finished. You can imagine."

"Unfair to Celts," said Megan. "Racist. We had middens, and—"

"Yes, just outside the front door. We saw those, too. . . ." Ann turned a laughing face to me. "Dr. Fenemore, would you like to come with us? We'd love you to, and you

can tell Megan all about her wretched broch.
She's been reading them up for days."

"Yes, do!" Megan joined her plea to
Ann's, with such eager sincerity that I
laughed and agreed.

"I'd love to. But Megan can do the lec-
turing. I don't know the first thing about
brochs. Look, why not come down to my
cottage now, and we'll have lunch there—I
never have much more than just a picnic
myself—then we can go across this afternoon, and maybe take tea to have on the
island? But on one condition, that you stop
calling me 'Dr. Fenemore.' We're a long way
from Cambridge now, and my name is
Rose."

We shared our resources for lunch—the
girls' picnic sandwiches and a cold pie and
some fruit I had bought that morning—and
ate it comfortably in the cottage kitchen,
with its grandstand view of the bay. To our
delight we also got a grandstand view of the
original owners of the bay—the otters. An
adult, presumably the female, came close
inshore, followed by two young ones, and
she seemed to be teaching them to fish, but
after a few splashing sallies with no success
she gave up, and dived away. The pups

slithered out onto the weedy boulders, not forty feet from the cottage window, and waited expectantly until she reappeared carrying a sizable fish, which the two of them ate together, wrestling over it among the sea-tangle. Then the three of them swam away into the deeper water under the headland.

"They'll come back," I said comfortingly to the girls, who were lamenting that they had forgotten to bring a camera. "Surely they will. This isn't called Otters' Bay for nothing. And if they come when my brother's here, he'll get some marvellous shots of them, I promise you, telephoto lens, the lot, and I think he's got a video camera now, too. He'll make prints for you. Now, anyone for coffee?"

"It is thought by some," said Megan, in a smooth lecturer's voice from which all trace of her faint Welsh lilt had vanished, "that the Scottish brochs may be an extension of the southern round-house culture, as exemplified in some sites of south-western England, but this seems unlikely, in view of—"

"The Scots'll be pleased to hear that,"

said Ann. "But I'm not just enthralled, and I'm sure Dr.—I'm sure Rose isn't, either."

"Do I really sound like that?" I asked.

Megan gasped and went scarlet. "It wasn't—I didn't—"

Then she saw me laughing and flopped her hands forward in a gesture of relief. "Of course you don't! I was quoting, anyway. I've been reading up on brochs, but when you're actually there it's really just the setting that's so marvellous, and trying to imagine the sort of life they lived."

"Raw shellfish for breakfast," muttered Ann.

She was ignored. "Weren't they really forts?" I asked. "Defensive places?"

"Yes. They must have been the Iron Age equivalent of the medieval castle with the village and everything clustered round. You can see where there could have been some buildings outside the main ring wall. Hey, Ann, be careful! Where d'you think you're going?"

Ann was already half way up the primitive stairway, a series of flat stones jutting out from the inner surface of the highest section of wall. "To look at the view. It's quite safe.

They're solid. Come on up." And Megan
went, as she always went where Ann led.

As she had said, there was really nothing
left here but the view, and the girls were ex-
claiming over it now, talking eagerly, and
pointing. I left them to it and made my way
along the inner side of the curving wall towards the doorway. This high western section was remarkably well preserved, the
stone slabs tightly laid, and the primitive
stairway safe and solid. But apart from this
the broch wall showed only as a circle of
raised turf, with a tumble of stones here and
there. Outside the circle a few mounds and
stones were all that remained of the huddle
of huts that had once crowded under the
broch's protection. Nettles grew everywhere, and ragwort, and the wall itself was
thick with plants growing in every available
gap. I saw saxifrages and wild thyme and
others that were unfamiliar to me. There was
a lot of some sort of stonecrop, which was
pretty enough but smelled at close quarters
rather like cleaning fluid.

The girls were still on their perch. I called
out: "I'm going over to look at the birds,"
and left them to it.

From what Neil had told me over supper

last night, I knew that the main bird colonies were on the western side of the island, where the cliffy coastline was cut into deep gullies, some of them sheer, and some filled with tumbles of massed boulders. I walked across that way, over the crest of the island, easy walking on wind-swept turf which in a short distance sloped gently down towards the head of the cliffs, where clouds of sea-birds were already wheeling and screaming at my approach.

There was a long promontory thrusting out to sea, with a deep inlet to either side where the tide sucked and swirled among fallen rocks. Above the water the cliffs rose sheer, but seamed with ledges and tufted with sea-pink and white campion. The birds were there.

I had never seen a big sea-bird colony before. The noise was horrendous, and the depths in front of me, filled with whirling wings, was frightening. I backed a step or two and sat down. Automatically—the writer's habit—I was trying to find the right word to describe the scene. The one I came up with eventually was "indescribable."

I gave it up and sat still, content to watch. No rare birds; just the incredible numbers, and the variety. Every niche of the craggy cliff held a nest, every hollow of the turfy ledge just below me had eggs or young gulls nestling there. Further down I saw kitti-wakes, with their gentle dark eyes and neat nests; below them, in deeper crevices, the ugly shags with their uglier young, showing the brilliant apricot gape of their beaks as they craned for food. Here and there, un-perturbed, solitary among the crowd, the fulmars; and out there in the air, huge and unmistakable among the teeming thou-sands, those unpleasant predators the great black-backed gulls, with their cruel beaks and dead eyes like shark's eyes, and their ineffable grace of flight.

The girls arrived then, breathless and laughing, and making sounds of disgust at the pervading smell and slime of birds' droppings.

"And to think the stuff's valuable!" That was Ann. "Guano at how many thousand pounds a ton . . . What a job! I wonder what they pay the chaps that shovel it up? Why don't they make an industry of it here? I'm sure there's just as much on these islands as there is in Peru or wherever. . . . No, don't tell me. It's a bit vertical, isn't it? Do you mind if we move back a bit? I don't normally mind heights, but this is different."

We retreated to the crest of the island, and sat down where the turf was clean and dry. Megan unpacked the picnic tea and handed me a plastic cup.

"Would you like a biscuit? We've got ginger snaps and shortbread." Her eyes were shining. "What a wonderful place! You'd think that with all those wings the island itself would start to fly!"

"Like that one in *Gulliver,*" said Ann, and this started a discussion as to whether Scotland could engineer the flight of its islands to hover over England and starve her of sunlight and rain, like Laputa in *Gulliver's Travels.* And this, in spite of some effort on my part to prevent it, led to the subject of science fiction, and where it had gone since the original efforts of Swift and Verne and H. G. Wells. But fortunately there would be no embarrassment: when Megan did eventually mention Hugh Templar, it was in passing, and with respect, along with John Wyndham and Arthur C. Clarke and Ursula Le Guin. Ann had never heard of any of them, and refused to be interested in a genre which she dismissed contemptuously as "fairy tales."

"But fairy tales were topical and highly moral," began Megan.

I had to intervene there. " 'Puss in Boots'? 'Jack the Giant Killer'? All those murderous little thugs in Grimm who cheated and stole and lied their way to the princess and half the kingdom? No, no, I know what you mean, and on the whole yes, you're right; your modern fairy tale—I don't just mean what's miscalled 'science fiction,' but all the stories that feed the modern hunger for the supernatural—they do tend to be more or less moral now. Surprisingly enough, considering the norm of fiction."

This steered them away, as I had meant it to, and they talked for a while longer, then fell silent, enjoying the warmth and the view.

Away to the west was the enormous glitter of the sea, where the small islands floated, weightless in the gently moving water. Even Mull, with its mountains, looked insubstantial. I could just make out Tobermory, looking like an Anne Redpath painting, cubes of white and blue and primrose and Venetian red, the houses and shops strung out along the bay, tiny in the distance.

"Can't see your cottage from here," said Ann. She had binoculars out and was looking the other way. "Can't really see that house, either; too many trees." She focussed nearer. "I wonder whose that tent is? No sign of them. Rather an odd place to camp, having to keep your eye on the tides the whole time."

"He's a geologist," I said. "I've met him. And he has a boat."

She lowered the glasses and glanced at her wrist. "And talking of watching the tides, it's nearly half past four, and Mrs. McD. does a high tea at half six. If we're to go home through the fields by the shore—what did you call them, Meg?"

"The machair. Yes, we ought to go. Can we get there along the shore from the causeway? Can you see? It looks as if there's a wall sticking right out over the shingle."

"That's the belvedere at the end of the House gardens," I said. "But there's a path round under the wall, and the machair starts just beyond the trees."

"Yes. You're right." Megan had the

glasses now. "That's fine, then, we'll go that way. . . . These are good glasses, Ann. I can just about see that b. and b. we had in Tobermory and—hang on a minute . . . I wonder? Yes, it could be . . ."

"What?" Ann and I spoke together.

"The *Stormy Petrel.* I'm sure it is."

"What?" My voice went high with excitement. "A stormy petrel? Where?"

"There. You see? That boat just out of Tobermory. You take a look, Ann." She handed the binoculars over. "Is it?"

"Wait a mo." Ann stood up and focussed. "I don't think—I can't quite—I honestly can't tell one boat from another, but it looks different. I think it's just a fishing boat."

I subsided onto the turf. "A boat . . . I thought you were talking about a bird, though how you'd spot one of those little things . . . Ah, well, skip it. What boat did you think it was? What's this *Stormy Petrel*?"

"Oh, it belongs to a terribly nice chap we met on Mull." Ann lowered the glasses. "No, he's not coming this way, so I can't get a close look, but I'm sure it's not him."

"Probably just as well, from what Mrs. McDougall told us," said Megan.

"Just what are you two talking about?

What has Mrs. McDougall got to do with it?" I asked.

"It's nothing, really. We met a chap the other day when we were staying near Dervaig, over the other side of Mull. We found a tiny b. and b. in a heavenly spot, a lovely bay and hardly any people. He had this boat called *Stormy Petrel* and he was living on it. Well, we sort of got together a couple of times—he was an interesting sort of man—done a lot of sailing, single-handed stuff. He'd even been round the Horn—"

"Had he indeed?" I sat up again, all interest now. "Sorry, go on, Ann."

"He did have some really good stories," said Ann, "and the way he told them—well, he was fun, and we both liked him. He took us out in his boat a couple of times, and he offered to take us over to the Treshnish Isles, but the forecast wasn't too good, so we never made it. He said he was coming to Moila later on, on business. He really was terribly nice, wasn't he, Megan?"

"Well, we thought so."

I looked from one to the other. "And Mrs. McDougall told you something about him that changed your minds?"

Ann said, judicially: "What she told us

doesn't alter the fact that he had bags of charm, but it seems that it's his—well, his stock-in-trade. . . . She knew him. She said he was from Moila, and ever since he was a boy he'd been a sort of con artist, and could get away with anything—"

"A pathological liar and a thief." Generations of Welsh Methodists spoke in Megan's direct voice. "What she told us meant just that, even though he was only a boy when she knew him. And as for sailing single-handed round the Horn—"

"We'd have been lucky to get as far as the Treshnish Isles," said Ann. "And Mrs. McD. was a bit staggered when we told her he was in Mull. Apparently everyone was hoping that he wouldn't come back here, because his people moved out after he went to prison, and asked Mrs. McD. not to let him know their address."

"He went to prison?" I caught Megan's quick glance, but Ann seemed to take my sharp interest for granted.

"Yes. She says he must have been released early, and she's dreading him coming to see her and demanding his parents' address. His name's Mackay, so if you should come across him—"

"Did she tell you what he'd been in prison for?"

"No. She rather skated away from the subject after a while."

"After she learned that you knew me and were coming to see me?"

They were gathering their things together, ready to go. They stopped and stared at me.

"Well, ye-es, I suppose it could have been. Ann?"

"I think so. Why, Rose? What's it got to do with you?"

I got to my feet. "Nothing, I hope," I said cheerfully. "Only that the Mackays used to live in my cottage. They moved away two years ago. That's all Mrs. McDougall told me. Perhaps she didn't want me to worry about it. In any case, she must have thought he was still safely locked away."

"Now that you know he's out—and around—will you mind being alone down there till Monday?"

"No. Now, don't worry about me. If you want to get back for your high tea, you'd better go."

"Aren't you coming over now?"

"Not straight away. There's time yet.

Come and see me again, won't you, and thanks for the tea."

"Thank *you* for the lunch," they said. "It's been a lovely day. Be seeing you!"

I watched them down to the causeway. Once across, they turned and waved, then were soon out of sight beyond the belvedere.

CHAPTER 12

After the girls had gone I sat for a little time, thinking.

What they had told me put quite a different complexion on the "mystery." I would have to seek Neil out and tell him that his old acquaintance was now, if not necessarily dangerous, at the least some kind of villain, who needed careful watching.

Neil had told me that he might spend the daytime hours between tides over here on Seal Island. He was working at present on the rocks at the north-west point, which were only accessible at low tide, or from a boat. I thought that, in spite of the noise of the birds, I would have heard a hammer going down there along the cliffs. In any case, there was not enough time left for me to go that way to look for him.

I made my way down towards the causeway Neil's rock, shaped like a shoe, was still
dry, the causeway exposed. I crossed carefully—even at low tide the seaweeds made
the stones treacherous—then went to the
boat-house window and peered in.

No boat. The place was empty. It was
also full of daylight: the angle at which it
stood to the water had made it impossible
to see from the islet, as I now saw, that the
doors were open.

Well, if he was out there hammering the
cliffs to bits, he would be back keeping
watch on the house tonight, and tomorrow
would be time enough, surely, to see him
and warn him? After all, he had known Ewen
Mackay as a boy, and was aware of the
reputation the latter had had even then. The
only new thing I could add was the prison
bit, and Mrs. McDougall had not told the
girls anything about the offense of which
Ewen had been convicted. I thought about
it as I walked up through the weedy garden.
Even if I had had pencil and paper on me,
I would not have cared to leave a note where
someone else might see it first. So tomorrow
would have to do, and the obvious move
now was to see Mrs. McDougall myself and

get what might be called hard evidence from her. She might be willing to give me, as the tenant of the former Mackay home, the details she had kept back from Ann and Megan. For my part I would have to decide how much I could tell her without giving away Neil's presence on Moila. I did not see how he could keep it secret for much longer, but that was his business.

However, after that visit to my cottage, Ewen Mackay was mine.

For form's sake, when I reached the house, I tried the french windows, then, round at the back, the door. All locked. I went home to the cottage, had an early supper, then set off on the walk to the post office.

The shop was shut, but the house door stood open. There was no sign of the girls, so I supposed they must have gone out again after their high tea. I met Morag on the step. She had been on an errand, she told me, and was it the telephone I needed? Her auntie was in, but I was to go at any time for the telephone. . . . Well, but her auntie would be pleased to see me. Any time. Please to come in. . . .

Mrs. McDougall was in her kitchen, not baking this time, though a pleasant after-smell of cooking pervaded the room. She was sitting beside the stove, knitting. She made me welcome, and nodded me to a chair on the other side of the stove. Morag unpacked her "errand," which was a large cauliflower from someone's garden, and a couple of pounds of tomatoes which had obviously, from the scent, been freshly picked; then, after we had admired them, left us.

"Tomatoes already?" I was actually fairly ignorant about the timing of tomatoes, or indeed, of any home-grown vegetables. But in view of the admiration that had obviously been expected, it was the right thing to say.

"My sister," said Mrs. McDougall. "Duncan—that's her man—spends near all his time on the garden when he's not fishing. They have a greenhouse, and he keeps adding to that—he's a handy man, is Duncan—and they are always earlier than anyone else around here." She reached the end of a row, paused for a moment to count, then turned her knitting and started again. "He comes from Achiltibuie, and worked for a bit at the hydroponics there. So now he's trying the same way here. Have you been there? I have not, but my sister worked in a hotel there for a time—that is where they met—and she says it is very remarkable."

I said no, I hadn't, and what were hydroponics? She told me, while the kettle sang gently on the top of the stove, and the creamy Aran knitting grew perceptibly on her lap. What she told me about vegetable growing meant very little to me, so I can barely recall now what was said, except that she would let me have some strawberries on Monday for my brother's supper, but I remember how easily the talk went, my unexpected visit serenely taken for granted, with no query as to why I had come. Just a pleased acceptance of the company, and a chat while the kettle sang its way to the boil.

It boiled, and she laid the knitting aside and made tea. From a tin in the cupboard scones were produced, and spread with butter and honey. I accepted plate and cup, thanked her, and wondered how on earth, into a conversation which had ranged from hydroponics to knitting to the situation in the smaller countries of the Warsaw Pact to the best breed of wool for spinning tweed to the honey and the siting of the hives—how on earth I could decently introduce my queries about Ewen Mackay.

I need not have worried. What I was experiencing was an islander's version of the tea-ceremony and its ritual. As she took her own cup and settled herself again in her chair, Mrs. McDougall looked at me over her spectacles and said comfortably:

"The girls will have told you about Ewen Mackay."

"Yes, they did."

"And I think that Archie told you that your cottage used to be where his family lived. So perhaps you are worried in case he comes home, now that he is back in these parts." It was a statement, not a question.

I hesitated, then shook my head. "Not really. But I did feel I'd like to know a bit more about him. Why he went to jail, for instance. Was it for something he did up here—in the islands?"

"No. It was in London."

"But his parents still lived here then?"

"They did. And of course everyone knew all about it, just as they knew that the Mackays, poor souls, had done everything they could for the boy ever since they took him in for adoption." She sipped tea. "You know that they left Moila. It was partly for shame after all the talk and the things that the papers said, but as well as that, they wanted to cut him off for good." A little smile. " 'For good.' That is exactly what it was. He was bad all through, that one, and they were good folk. They wanted rid of him for good, and I think they were a bit afraid he might come back, and then how could they turn him out?"

"Afraid of him? Of violence, you mean?"

"I do not know. I did hear once that he had threatened his father, but I do not know if this is true, and they, poor souls, never said a word against him."

"Mrs. McDougall," I said flatly, "what was he sent down for?"

She set her cup aside and picked up her knitting again. "Miss Fenemore, they do say that if a man has done wrong, and has been punished for it, that should be the end of it. Do you not agree? It is true the man is bad, but he has done two years, almost, in prison. It might be better to forget it." The needles clicked. "No, do not look like that, lassie. I'm not calling shame on you. I blame myself for talking to those other lassies. I would have done better to have held my tongue."

"You did hold your tongue. You said nothing to me. You only let it out to the girls because you got a shock when they said they'd seen him, and you were afraid yourself that he might come here and demand his parents' address from you. Isn't that true?"

"Aye, it's true. Not 'afraid,' though. There's no harm could come to me here, with good neighbours round and about all the while. And he'd not offer harm to me, I think. But you, lassie"—once more I was promoted from "Miss Fenemore"—"there's no need for you to fear him coming to the cottage, even though he has a boat and could get into the bay without anyone seeing him. He'll have been told, for sure, that his folk are gone, and the place is let."

"Yes. Well . . . Thank you for the tea, Mrs. McDougall. It's been lovely talking with you, but if I'm to get home . . ." I rose. "Since I'm here, may I use the telephone, please, before I go?"

"You may." The knitting was in her lap and she was regarding me steadily over the spectacles. "Just sit you down again for a minute, lassie. It wasn't just for idleness that you came to ask about that rapscallion, was it? Are you afraid to sleep in that cottage? Because if you are—"

"No, it's all right. It's not that."

She nodded. "I thought so. It is something else." Silence for a minute. She seemed to be deciding something about the knitting in her lap. Then she said, with apparent irrelevance: "Those two lassies, they think the world of you."

I could think of nothing to say to that, so I said nothing.

She nodded again, as if I had answered her. "Very well, I will tell you what you ask me, and I do not want to know why you ask it." She picked up her knitting again, and the needles clicked. "It came out in the court that he had been robbing old ladies . . . confidence trickster was the word. He would watch the notices in the papers, and when someone died and the widow was left alone, he would go there and think up some sort of lie—he lied always, as a boy, even when there was no need, and he looked so clean and innocent that if you did not know him you would believe him, every time. And sometimes even though you did know

him . . . So he would use the charm and the
lies on the old lady in her grief, and cheat
her out of everything he could get. The one
they took him for in the end, she was eighty-
five years old, and ailing, and he robbed her
of her life-savings, and that was less than
three hundred pounds. He would spend that
much, they said, in a week. He pleaded
guilty to three other offenses. Do you see
what I mean about shame?"

"Yes, I see." I was thinking hard. Should
I tell her here and now that Ewen Mackay
had already been to the cottage? It was
possible that his return to Moila had been
sparked by the notice in the papers of Mrs.
Hamilton's death. He had been in jail when
that occurred. On his release he had come
straight up to Moila, and by last weekend—
it was possibly true enough—had not heard
of his parents' departure, but had thought
he could go straight home. And then what?
There was no elderly widow to con, but
there was an empty house, and one he knew
well. He must know, at least casually, what
there was of value there. So, no con-tricks
needed here, just a simple robbery? But his
luck was out, in that the new owner, who
was no old lady, but a sufficiently able-

bodied young man, was here before him.
And knew him.

And Neil, for his part, knew that if anyone
on Moila heard of his, Neil Hamilton's, return, the news would fly around and certainly reach Ewen Mackay. So, since for the
present Neil preferred to lie low and find out
just what Ewen was up to, I could not tell
Mrs. McDougall of Ewen's night-time visit.
If I could not reassure her by telling her Neil
was there, and watching, it was possible—
more, probable—that she would insist either
on my moving into a lodging in the village,
or that some of the men from the village
would keep watch on Otters' Bay and the
empty house.

I would have to talk to Neil first. Tomorrow. Tonight all I could do was make sure
of Crispin. I thanked Mrs. McDougall again
and went to the telephone.

The hospital answered, with cheering
news. It seemed that my brother would soon
be on his way. He had left that morning, to
stay with his Glasgow friends; and yes, he
had left the Glasgow number in case I
should call.

I called, and Crispin answered, so cheerfully that I knew all was well.

"Yes, I'm all set to come up tomorrow. We'll be at the Columba Hotel, and on the ferry first thing Monday."

"We?"

"Yes, there was someone else heading for Oban, and we were in the crash together. He'll be getting the same train. To tell you the truth, I'm quite glad of his help. I'm what they laughingly call mobile, but carrying a suitcase, as well as all my camera junk, is a little beyond me as yet."

"But the foot really is mending?"

"It's fine. Another day or two and I'll be skipping like a ram on the high hills. Depending, of course, on what you've got laid on for me. Anything new?"

"Only several hundred thousand gulls and shags and things. But I did see black guillemots swimming down in the bay, and a gully full of boulders where they probably nest."

"Sounds great. Accessible?"

"From the sea. And there's a boat handy. Don't forget the binocs."

"Is it likely? Anything else you need me to bring? The local supermarket's open on Sundays now, and Laura's going there in the morning, she tells me."

"Nothing I can think of, unless you want something fancy in the way of cheeses. Can't get those here. Oh, and some cream, too. You're getting strawberries for supper on Monday."

"Good heavens. The only ones I've seen here are from California, and they don't taste like the real thing at all. What are the Hebrides coming to? Greenhouse effect?"

"No. We've got hydroponics. I must go now. I've got a long, lonely road home in front of me. Good night, Cris."

"Good night. Take care, and *hasta la vista.*"

We rang off.

Nearly ten o'clock, and still light. I saw no one on the long lonely road home, and the only enemy that attacked me was the midges.

CHAPTER 13

I slept later than usual next morning, and woke to see half past nine on my bedside clock, and a cascade of raindrops chasing each other down the window. By the time I had had breakfast and done the morning's chores it was after eleven and, though the rain was letting up, it was still wet enough to keep anyone indoors who didn't have to go out.

I decided that I didn't have to go out. It was not a hard decision to take. Rationalized, it meant that Neil already knew enough about Ewen Mackay's record, and of course he was already on the watch for any more suspicious moves. If he, Neil, was content to leave the house unwatched by day, and to spend his time looking at rocks on the broch island, then I could stay indoors with

a clear conscience, and wait for the rain-
storm to pass.

I got back to work, by which I mean that
I got my papers and notes out, and then sat
looking at them for what seemed like a
dreary lifetime, and was really probably only
twenty minutes. The words I had written—
and had almost, in the interval, forgotten—
mocked me and were meaningless. My
notes told me what was to happen next, but
my brain no longer knew how to move plot
and people forward. Block. Complete block.
I sat and stared at the paper in front of me
and tried to blank out the present and get
back into my story—forward, that is, into my
invented future, and out of the world of queries and vague apprehensions.

From experience, I knew what to do. Write.
Write anything. Bad sentences, meaningless
sentences, anything to get the mind fixed
again to that sheet of paper and oblivious of
the "real" world. Write until the words begin
to make sense, the cogs mesh, the wheels
start to turn, the creaking movement quick-
ens and becomes a smooth, oiled run, and
then, with luck, exhaustion will be forgotten,
and the real writing will begin. But look up
once from that paper, get up from the table

to make coffee or stir the fire, even just raise your head to look at the view outside the window, and you may as well give up until tomorrow. Or for ever.

It was the rain that saved me. I could not have looked out of the window if I had tried, the chores were all done, and there was nothing whatever to do except sit at that table and write.

I wrote. A year or so later, or it may have been an hour, I crumpled up four sheets of paper and threw them to the floor, and started another, and I was there. And in another light-year or two I was through the word-barrier, and the book had suddenly reached the stage—the wonderful moment to get to—where I could walk right into my imaginary country and see things that I had not consciously created, and listen to people talking and watch them moving, all apparently independent of me.

I came out of it and saw the window clear and the sun shining and the heavy clouds rolled back to leave a blue, washed sky. I could hear gulls crying, and the soft, flattened whispering of the sea. My watch said twenty past one.

Scrambled eggs again, and coffee, then

I made a thermos of tea, pushed that, with
a packet of biscuits, into the pocket of my
anorak, and set off along the cliff path.

It was half past two by my watch when I
reached the Hamilton house. I went to the
back door—still fast shut—and knocked.
The sound echoed through the silence with
that hollow, unmistakably empty noise. Perhaps he was working on the island again. I
made my way round the house and crossed
the mossy terrace to look in through the
drawing-room window. Nobody there, of
course. It looked just the same. If he was
really living in the house he must be taking
pains to leave no signs of his occupancy.
Somehow the knowledge irked me. He had
been right, I thought; in spite of what the
girls and Mrs. McDougall had told me, the
whole idea of a "mystery" was, in this place,
wrong and irritating. Whatever Ewen Mackay was up to, it could really hardly matter.
Must not be allowed to matter. He no longer
belonged here. Had never belonged. He
was the changeling of the classic tale, thrust
on good people, who was to repay good
with evil. The hints he had thrown out, that
he was connected in some illegitimate way

with the Hamilton family, could be dismissed as a typical lie told to impress, another Cape Horn. I wondered what his real origins were, and if there really was such a thing as original sin, people born evil. It was fashionable not to think so, but there were people of whom it had to be believed. For instance—

I checked the train of thought. This was no place for it. Moila was too lovely, and my ivory tower was still solid. This was my holiday, and my brother would be here tomorrow, and all would be normal once more.

The boat-house was empty again, its seadoors fastened back. I walked to the end of the pier and looked across at the island. There was no sign of life except the birds, and Neil's tent was again fastened shut. I glanced at my watch. The tide was still falling, and should be safe for another three hours or so. I went across.

I climbed the slope to the hollow where Neil's tent was pitched. There was no sign of him there. I stood still, listening. No sound of a hammer. There were gulls flying and calling, but I had not disturbed the main colony, and I thought that I would have heard if he had been working below the cliffs at the northwest point. I gave it a couple of minutes, then made for the broch and the steps up to the landing where the girls had gone yesterday.

The steps looked fragile, transverse slabs of stone with one end built into the dry-stone structure of the curving wall, and jutting into the air with no other support. But they were solid, and led safely up to the ruined top of the wall where another, larger slab made a good viewpoint. From here I found, as I had hoped, that I could see down to the shore at the point where Neil had told me he wanted to work. If he had been close to the cliff I would not have been able to see him, but I could see the whole section of shoreline, and there was no boat there. Short of clambering down there myself I could be no surer, and there was no real need for that. More rationalization. I made my way carefully down the staircase, intending to sit in the sun at the foot of the wall and drink my tea, but the breeze could find no way there, and the strange, musky smell from the wall where those plants grew was stronger than ever. Besides, the midges were out. I left the broch and walked uphill as far as I could without disturbing the bird colony, then made my way towards the southern end of the island, where the land sloped gradually down to the sea in long, flat terraces of rock. I found a niche where a small landslide had left a level lawn with a backing of turf, and where the breeze still moved enough to allay the midges, and sat down to my picnic.

The silence—for the sound of birds and sea adds up to silence as beautifully as we ever know it in the noisy world of today— together with the sweetly moving air, and the scents of thyme and bell-heather and sun-warmed bracken, all combined to distill something very potent. It was the sort of time and place where one might have ex- pected an idea, the spring of a poem to well up from the quiet and the beauty. But sheer sensation—the warmth of the sun, the scent of the air, the mundane pleasure of tea and biscuits—simple well-being possessed me so that I could only feel, not think. A look at the sea below me told me that the tide was still low, though presumably it had begun to turn. A glance at my watch showed that it was still only ten past five. I leaned back

again, shut my eyes, and let the sun have
its way.

Gradually, as the breeze moved and ed-
died, I became conscious of a strange, soft
sound that was filling the air. It was like the
sound of the sea, but it was not the sea. It
was like the wind, but was not the wind. It
was as if sea and wind together were singing a lament, mourning with a not quite human voice, the voice of water echoing in a
sea-cave, weird, unearthly.

I opened my eyes and sat up to listen,
with the skin furring up on my arms.

Teach me to hear mermaids singing . . .

The wonderful thing about literature is
that great poetry can chime in on any
thought or experience. As Donne's line rang
in my head I placed the sound. Something
Neil had told me about the island. This was
Eilean na Roin, the Island of the Seals, and
the grey seals came ashore here to breed
and to bask. And now, perhaps, with the
evening tide coming in, the seals had come
with it, and were singing.

It is no wonder that, hearing that uncanny
sound coming out of the mist, the old sailors

ascribed it to mermaids or sirens or strange creatures of the deep. It is almost music, almost a human sound, but never quite. It is as if a wind instrument, soulless in itself, were being played through warm and breathing tissues instead of through wood or metal. And it is magical, compelling wonder. For me, it was the peak of a perfect day I had done some good writing, and I had heard mermaids singing.

Very slowly, and keeping down below the seals' horizon, I crept forward towards the sound of singing. At last I gained the crest of a rise, and there below me stretched the sloping flat rocks, and yes, the mermaids were there, their fur dry in the sun, their bodies slack and contented, their eyes closed, enjoying the afternoon, exactly as I had done myself. A fat grey mermaid, waving her flippers gently, turned on her back to show a pale, spotted stomach. Another came heaving out of the sea and flopped to where her calf lay, and, delightfully, the baby nuzzled in to suck. Not very far from me another baby lay, apparently full fed and contented. It saw me, and the big eyes stared with mild curiosity, but without fear. This was Eilean na Roin, and I was only a passer-by.

It was time to go. Reluctantly, I inched backwards without disturbing the sleeping nursery, and stood up. I took another glance at my watch. Ten past five.

Ten past five?

It had been ten past five when I had last checked on the time.

I held the watch to my ear—it was battery-run, but a faint tick could normally be heard. No sound. And now that I thought about it, I had vaguely wondered at the "good time" I had made on my walk from the cottage, and at the leisurely stretch of time I had had on the island. Had I even left my cottage at two o'clock? My watch must have been gradually slowing to a stop all day.

I ran.

I could still see the causeway. I could also see the rock that Neil had pointed out to me, still half out of water. It was all downhill to the causeway, and the turf was smooth. I would make it.

I had forgotten the other thing that Neil had told me.

"The tide," he had said, "comes in like a horse trotting."

And it did. Though the marker stone had been half out of water when I started to run, the whole barrage of banked stones, with the causeway atop, was suddenly aswirl, and as I raced for the crossing, the level seemed to rise a foot or more.

I stood hesitating. I could probably still have got across, but as I have said, the stones of the causeway were thick with seaweed, and treacherous even when exposed. And though I can swim pretty well, the swirl of the tide was fierce, and looked dangerous; and besides, I had no desire to swim.

And of course the moments of dismay and indecision were moments lost. The next wave came round the point, and the marker vanished. So that was that. And the tide would be high at what? Midnight?

I had a few moments of fury, a fury compounded of shame at my own stupidity, the triteness of the situation, the thought of my cottage and supper and the cozy fire-side. Then the fury faded. Other pictures took the place of these; Neil's tent, not far up the brae, and the possibility not only, at worst, of having its shelter for the night, but of my seeing from that vantage point when Neil came back with his boat. If so, and if I could attract his attention, he would surely bring the boat over for me.

I trudged up to the camp-site again, to find that there was no need even to look for drift-wood for a fire. Inside that stout little tent was a very efficient "camping-gas" burner, complete with kettle, billycan, matches, tea bags, and powdered milk. And investigating Neil's stores I found baked beans, sardines, a couple of small tins of ham, and some crispbread. Like the Swiss Family Robinson, I had very little to complain about. There was also, of course, a good sleeping-bag. I only hoped, as the sun sank lower and the breeze grew cool, that I was not going to be obliged to use it.

The seals sang until sunset, and then fell silent.

As dusk drew in, the air emptied of birds, and gradually they, too, fell silent. Only the tide, full and flowing, filled the half-light of the Highland night with its cold sound. I could no longer distinguish the house, and even the boat-house, much nearer, was lost in the shadows. But no boat came in.

Long before the sky dimmed enough to let the stars through, I lighted the gas burner and ate baked beans off a paper plate and finished off with tea and biscuits. Then I got into the sleeping-bag.

CHAPTER 14

I had gone to sleep with the sound of the sea filling the night with subdued song. What woke me was the land singing.

At first it was part of a dream, which vanished as soon as I woke and knew that I was alone on the broch island, lying on the turf in a sleeping-bag, with my head pillowed on my rolled-up sweater, but seemingly connected with the earth itself, from which, apparently right below my head, came a sound every bit as strange as the mermaids' song of the seals.

It was a soft, slow moaning, punctuated with sharp little sounds like cries; the earth grieving in a whisper, but in some weird way with a purpose as if this were a language, a communication. Crooning would be the better word for it, and as the word suggested itself I had a swift and vivid mental picture of the colony of birds on the west of the island, birds aggressive, protective, maternal, tender.

Weird, perhaps, but not frightening. I sat up. The sound retreated, but still it was there, somewhere in the night, as if thrumming along some wire sunk in the ground. I slid out of the sleeping-bag and unzipped the tent opening. I stuck my head out and looked around me.

Twilight still, no more than that. The sky was clear, greyed over, with stars. The moon, a half moon polished thin at the edges, swam low and gave a little light. My world, the island, was drained of colour, but every shape was clear. Nothing stirred, no bird cried. But still, faint now but persistent, came that crooning subterraneous song. Then all at once, so subtly that I could hardly be sure when I first saw it, I realized that the sky was full of movement, small shadowy shapes skimming low over the ground, silently, as if bats or night-time swallows were criss-crossing my line of vision, swarming between the broch and the sea.

The stormy petrels. Mother Carey's chickens. The fragile, tiny black birds, nocturnal and solitary, that come ashore to nest, but spend most of their lives flying close above the sea-waves, come storm or shine. They must be nesting in the rabbit-holes beneath the turf where the tent was pitched, and in the broch, where the queer chemical smell I had noticed came not from the plants but from the holes where the birds sat on their eggs.

If anything had been needed to crown my day, this would have been it. To be here, alone in the Highland night, and to witness the flight of these marvellous creatures, so shy, so rarely seen . . . I found I was outside the tent, standing up with my jacket clutched to me, the better to see them. They took no notice of me; they were creatures of the night, the air, and the ocean, and I was only a piece of the land, meaningless, to be flown round like a boulder or a stump of wood.

I was brought back to the mundane present by the shiver of chill that ran over me. Pulling my coat more closely round me, I turned my attention from the dark shape of the broch and its flitting ghosts to my own situation. I looked across to where the Hamilton house must stand in its shadows. No light there. But that, of course, meant nothing. Even if Neil had returned while I had been asleep, he would take care not to show a light.

More importantly, somewhere in the early morning hours the tide was due to turn. I had no way of telling what time it was, but surely it might soon be possible for me to escape from my desert island and make my way back to the cottage and a warm bed.

I was not familiar enough, yet, with the light nights of the Highlands to be able to guess at the time, but the sky was paler, and the stars were fading. I took a few cautious steps forward to where, by craning, I could just make out the ghostly crescent of the beach opposite the pier. I could not see the state of the causeway.

Then suddenly, I heard it. A boat's engine, throttled back and purring softly, somewhere beyond the headland to the east. Neil, coming back to keep the promised watch on his house. And from where? Fishing?

At that moment, all that this suggested to me was the possibility of fresh mackerel for breakfast. . . .

I dived back into the tent and scrambled

into my sweater and shoes. I did zip the tent flap shut, but wasted no other time on housekeeping; I would come back in daylight to tidy up and replace the stores I had used. It was not possible to hurry downhill in that half-light, so I made myself go slowly, and at last reached the beach and the end of the causeway.

It was almost uncovered. Almost—but I could just make out a narrow stretch half way over where the water flowed smooth and fast with each swell. As I craned to see, the next wave broke and swirled, luminous with foam. Even if I failed to attract Neil's attention, I would probably be able to cross quite soon.

I found that I could no longer hear the boat's engine. I knew very little about boats, and had hated what little experience of sailing I had had, but it seemed unlikely that any boat would shut down its engine until it was safely round into the bay, or even then. I strained to hear, and had just decided that it would be difficult to hear an idling motor over the lap and rush of the sea in the channel, when I saw the light.

Not a boat's riding light; this was the small, dodging light of an electric torch coming round the path that skirted the headland. It was the path from my cottage, and I remembered the little cove called Half-way House, a cove where in any weather a boat might tie up safely and its owner make his way round to Taigh na Tuir. Its owner who did not want, or did not dare, to bring his boat round to the jetty? Not Neil, then. Someone else who did not want his visit known. Ewen Mackay.

The mackerel disappeared from the breakfast table, and the mystery came back with a rush. It was certainly Ewen Mackay. I could see him now, outlined fairly clearly against the light background of the beach, as the torch-beam cleared the path and he came fast along the shore towards the boat-house.

I sat down on the sand, in the darkness cast by a large boulder. He would never see me unless I moved. He was at the boat-house. A flash of the torch again, as if to check that no boat was there, then he turned to face the causeway, took some-thing from a pocket and raised what were apparently night-glasses to his eyes. I froze in the shelter of my rock, but the glasses were aimed higher, at the tent. I had a momentary qualm; what would he read into the carefully closed flaps? That Neil was not sleeping there after all, or merely that he shut the flaps at night against the midges or the weather? I supposed, since to him Neil was only "John Parsons," it did not matter either way, and if Ewen saw the little pile of debris—tins and used paper plates and my thermos—that I had left outside the tent, it would surely go to persuade him that Neil was safely ensconced on the island.

But, unfortunately, Neil was not even safely ensconced in the house, as he should have been, so Ewen Mackay was free to resume whatever his business had been there on Wednesday night. And with no witness but me.

I sat very still. He turned away, apparently satisfied, then pushed the glasses back into his pocket, flashed the torch briefly down at the rough stones of the pier, and went away with long strides in the direction of the house.

The next wave broke with a crash and a swirl and a dangerous-looking suck of water back into the channel. Not this time. Nor next. Nor the time after, I thought, even if the causeway came clear. There was no way

I was going across to follow Ewen Mackay to spy on his activities at the house. If he really had left his boat in the cove round the point, he would have to come this way again, and I would certainly be able to see if he brought anything with him. I hugged my jacket close round me, and waited.

It seemed a very long time before he came back. The tide had cleared the causeway, and it was perceptibly lighter, when he came out through the stone arch of the garden gate. He carried what looked like a bag, bulging with something, over one shoulder. He made his way rapidly to the boathouse—there was no need, now, for the torch—and disappeared behind it. Almost at once he reappeared, without the bag, and set off again, walking fast, for the house.

I stood up, the better to see the state of the causeway, and made some rapid calculations. Though it was now possible to cross, the central stones were still wet, and in that poor light would be treacherous. It was an easy decision to make. Sensibly, I decided to wait and see.

Which was just as well, as this time he came back after a very few minutes. He was carrying a flat, square object which looked heavy. When he had left that, too, behind the boat-house, he emerged stretching his arms as if in relief, as he stood once more scanning the bay and the shadowy slopes of the broch island.

And that seemed to be it for the night. He vanished behind the boat-house, and when I saw him again he was aiming fast for the cliff path, with the bag once more slung over his shoulder. I watched him round the end of the point and out of sight, then ran for the causeway.

I got across without mishap, and was at the back of the boat-house within seconds. The square object was there, leaning against the wall. It looked, in that half-light, like a big framed picture, propped up with its face to the wall.

It *was* a picture. I tilted it to see. A portrait, unglazed, in oils, with a heavy, ornate frame. The portrait of a man, not young, in country tweeds, with a gun over his shoulder and a spaniel at heel. I did not know enough about painting to recognize it, or even guess at its value, but in the present-day crazy art market even a relatively modern painting might well be very valuable, and this one was ap-

parently worth the trouble and risk that
Ewen Mackay had taken. I toyed with the
idea of taking it myself, and hiding it somewhere, but it was almost too heavy for me
to carry, and there was nowhere much
nearer than the house itself where it could
be hidden. The boat-house was too obvious, and anywhere in the woods or garden
was still wet with the night's dew. Besides,
the move would hardly help, only alert him
and start him searching, not just for the picture, but for whoever had moved it.

In any case, no need. I took a quick
breath of relief as I heard it; the engine of
another boat, throttling down to a murmur
as she crept into the bay.

This time I waited to make sure before I
ventured out on the jetty, but it was Neil's
boat, and Neil himself standing ready to
step out of it as it nosed in alongside the
landing-place.

CHAPTER 15

I ran to him, stumbling and nearly falling on the rough stones of the jetty. He jumped out of his boat and caught my arm to steady me.

"*Rose?* Rose! What on earth are you doing here?"

"Sh! Keep your voice down! He's been here again. I saw him go up to the house—"

"Hang on. Take it easy. You're shaking. . . . Why, you're cold—"

"I'm not cold. I'm all right. Neil, it's Ewen Mackay. I saw him—never mind how, I'll tell you later, but the point is, he's been up to the house and taken things. Brought them down here and then gone off along the cliff path with them. He'll be coming back, because he left something here—"

"Along the cliff path? Did you hear a boat?"

"Yes. I thought he must have left it in that place round the point, Halfway House. Did you see anything as you came in?"

"No, but you can't see into that cove from the way I came. But what are you doing here? No, that can wait. You say you saw him go up to the house and take something? You mean you actually saw him breaking in?"

"No. I was over on the island. I saw him take a look at the boat-house first, then, when I suppose he saw you weren't home, he went up towards the house, and after a bit he came back with a bag, you know, like Santa Claus, slung over his shoulder. It looked like that duffel bag of yours, and it was heavy. He dumped it down behind the boat-house and went back towards the house, then after a bit he came down again with a picture, and dumped that, then he took the bag and made off up the path with it."

"Hold on a minute. A *picture*?"

"Yes. A big one. It's behind the boat-house, there. I took a look at it."

"There's no picture in the house worth stealing." He moved quickly to knot the boat's rope through a ring sunk in the jetty. "Let's have a look. Maybe there was one I didn't know about. . . . Good God!"

"Do you know it?"

"I should. It's Great-Uncle Fergus."

"Valuable?"

"Good heavens, no. Not even good, apparently, though it's very like him, and dear old Sam—the dog—and Aunt Emily loved it. She used to say it was the best thing in the house. It was in her bedroom." He was looking around him as he spoke. "This was all? This and the duffel bag?"

"All I saw. I heard the boat, and then I saw him. He only made the two trips to the house."

"The duffel bag. Could he have been carrying guns—shotguns—in it?"

"I don't think so. Guns? You don't mean—?"

"Yes." His voice was grim. "I told you I was going to check the house. Uncle Fergus's guns have gone missing. I've been to the mainland to report it. So if he did take them, it must have been when he was here before."

"And they could be in his boat, couldn't they? Neil," I said, urgently, "he did take this picture tonight, and whatever he took it for, it's got to mean he'll be coming back for it, and soon. Look, if you put your boat into the boat-house now, he wouldn't see it till he got right down here again, and then perhaps—"

I stopped. Clear in the silence we heard an engine start.

Neil grabbed my arm again. "Quick. Get in. He's not coming back, he's running for it. He must have heard me. Come on!"

Somehow I was in the boat, and Neil had cast off and was edging her out from the jetty She backed in a gentle arc to face the open sea, and as Neil gunned the engine she jumped forward and then settled to a smooth, fast pace.

"There he is. No, there! You're too far out!" I had to shout it above the noise of the engine. I pointed to where, just visible against the dark background of the cliffs, the grey boat raced, the foam white under her bows and in her long wake.

Neil shook his head and made some gesture which I could not interpret, but as it was obvious that he, too, had seen *Stormy Petrel* and knew what he was about, I let it be. There were a hundred questions still to be asked and answered, but at this speed and in this noise speech was impossible. I hung on, keeping one eye on Neil in case I could help him, and the other on *Stormy Petrel.*

Now I thought I could see what Neil was trying to do. The two boats were running along the coastline on almost parallel courses, Ewen close in, perforce following the jagged line of the shore, and our boat (I found later that she was called *Sea Otter)* on a straight course some way out. When on two occasions Ewen turned to make for the open sea, Neil, increasing our speed slightly, held on to what looked like a collision course. Even though it must have been obvious that he would not hold to it at the last, the threat was enough to make *Stormy Petrel* veer again to her original course, and though she was trying to increase speed, and was perhaps a little more powerful than *Sea Otter,* we, on our straight line, could hold her comfortably.

We were almost round to Otters' Bay now. The headland looming ahead of us out of the growing daylight would be the one immediately to the west of the cottage. *Stormy Petrel* wheeled again towards us, and this time Neil gave her sea-room. In a moment I could see why. From the tip of the headland and for some way out to sea the waves were breaking white against half-submerged fangs and stacks of rock that had in time past broken away from the main cliffs. They were no real danger to anyone who knew the coast, and all the time the light was growing stronger. Ewen obviously knew his way, but although Neil gave him room he made no further attempt to break free, or even to reach open water. He slowed down to pick his way among the patches of white water quite close inshore, at one point even vanishing between a towering sea-stack and the main cliff; then, once past the headland, he throttled right back and motored tamely into Otters' Bay, making for the jetty there.

I turned in surprise to Neil, to see him pointing away from the bay towards where, in a cloud of spray, a powerful-looking launch was heading fast towards us. I had never seen a police launch, but this one had an unmistakably official look about it, and in size and speed would be more than a match for either *Stormy Petrel* or *Sea Otter.*

Ewen Mackay was still tying up when we nosed gently in to rub shoulders with

Stormy Petrel, and Neil jumped ashore and turned to hand me out.

"Why, Miss Fenemore! You were out with Mr. Parsons, then?" Ewen straightened with a look of surprise and pleasure. With dark hair rumpled by the wind, flushed face and those brilliantly blue eyes, he looked very handsome. His expression was one of un-complicated welcome, which altered as he turned to Neil. "Or is it Mr. Hamilton? Oh, yes, it took me a bit of time to recognize you, but I got there in the end. Did you have a good night's fishing? I've been out myself, and I didn't get a thing. Not a thing." Another glance at me, apparently quite free of guile. "Well, I'm glad he got you home safely . . . It seems you've forgotten how to handle a boat, Neil, all those years in Dismal Swamp with canoes and muggers and billabongs, whatever they may be. Just what the hell were you doing? A game's a game, but you could have piled me up back there, and then you'd have had a few questions to answer!"

"I have one to ask." Neil made no attempt at a normal tone. His was grim and totally unfriendly "Where are the guns?"

* * *

"Guns?" asked Ewen blankly. "What guns?"

It was some time later, and the scene had shifted to the cottage sitting-room which, with myself and the two men, and two large detectives, was rather crowded. Ewen had shown surprise, which of course looked genuine, when the launch, on coming along-side the jetty, turned out to belong not to the police but to Customs and Excise, who announced their intention of searching *Stormy Petrel,* while the detectives had "a few questions to ask." He did make the in-evitable protest of the recently released prisoner: was he to be hounded wherever he went, just because of the recent trip "abroad," and surely that debt was paid in full and he could be allowed to start again in, of all places, his old home, which he was only visiting in the hope of finding where his parents had moved to; to lose touch with his dear mother was not to be borne; he needed to talk with his parents, to explain things to them, and ask for their forgiveness. And why the Customs men anyway, and what on earth did they hope to find . . . ? And so on, still in that pleasant, reasonable voice, with eyes that were just guileless enough appealing for sense and clemency from his audience.

The official section of that audience was attentive but impartial. Far from hounding him gratuitously, they said, they were acting on information received. They would like to search his boat. No, they had no warrant, but they could take him and the boat back to Oban, where a warrant could be obtained. No objection? Then, sir, they were much obliged, and we'll leave it to you chaps while you, Jimmy, come with me to the cottage and talk with Mr. Mackay there.

Then, to me: "If we may? I understand that you have rented the cottage, miss. Miss Fenemore, isn't it?"

I said that it was, and they were welcome to come in. He thanked me, and introduced himself as Detective-Sergeant Fraser, and his companion as Detective-Constable Campbell.

I unlocked the door and led the way in. Ewen came, with a shrug and a smile and a lifted eyebrow, and the two detectives close behind him. Neil followed them in and shut the door. He was rather pale, and tended to watch the policemen rather than

Ewen. I noticed that Ewen did not look in his direction.

" 'On information received'?" he said, looking from one detective to the other. "From whom, and about what? It must be serious, to have brought you out on that TV-type chase? And why the Customs people? Just what is this all about?"

The sergeant consulted a notebook. "You hired the boat *Stormy Petrel* on June fifteenth from one Hector McGillivray of Uig on the island of Faarsay?"

"Yes. At least, I suppose it was the fifteenth. . . . It was three days after— Yes, the fifteenth. So what? I paid him, didn't I?"

"We have reason to believe," said the sergeant, taking no notice of the question, "that this boat has recently been involved in illegal traffic, and that the said operation was centered on the island of Faarsay."

"Illegal traffic?" Ewen looked taken aback, then he laughed. "Faarsay? Do you mean that old Hector's been poaching salmon again? But how does that affect me? I've only had the boat since the fifteenth, and before that I was—" A quick glance at me. "I don't need to tell you where I was, do I?"

Once again the sergeant ignored the question. He watched Ewen steadily, while the constable, who had seated himself at the kitchen table, was taking notes. I thought that Neil, still over by the door, had a puzzled look. He glanced from time to time out of the window, as if to see what was happening down at the jetty.

"Not salmon," said the sergeant, "no. That would not bring the Customs here. They are looking for drugs."

"*Drugs?*" This time, unmistakably, the shock was genuine. Ewen went as white as paper, and jerked upright in his chair. "Drugs? What are you talking about? What's it got to do with me? Do you mean that that bloody fool Hector McGillivray fobbed me off with a boat that's—that's been—?" He stopped abruptly, biting his lip. The two detectives watched him, unmoved. Ewen sat back in the chair, and managed, very creditably I thought, a wry little smile. "No wonder I got the damned boat cheaply," he said. "That comes of trusting chaps you've known all your life. Like Neil here. Well? Just when did all this so called traffic take place? While I was safely locked away, I hope? As far as I'm concerned, I went to Hector be-

cause I knew him and I knew he'd let me
have a boat cheaply, and I've used it since
then—since the fifteenth—for pleasure, and
now to come over and look my people up.
So the Customs can search all they like;
they won't find a thing." And he included
Neil, and then me, in the smile.

"Thank you, sir." The sergeant glanced
across at his colleague, saw him busily writing, then turned back to Ewen. "You must
understand that the boat's history is the affair of the Customs officers. They will talk
to you later. We have our own inquiries to
make. The launch gave us a lift over, to save
us waiting for the ferry in the morning, that
is all. But their search of your boat will save
us time, as well. We have been lucky there."

"Haven't you just?" said Ewen. "Search
for what, since you're not after all the heroin,
or whatever I'm supposed to have been fer-
rying around the islands for a week?"

"We have reason to believe that you recently broke into Taigh na Tuir, the house
belonging to Mr. Hamilton here, and that you
know something of the whereabouts of two
valuable guns."

"Guns?" repeated Ewen blankly "What

guns? And who gave you reason to believe—?"

"I did," said Neil.

The surprise and shock registered yet again on Ewen's face were so real that even I, if this time I had not known better, would have thought them genuine. He turned to face Neil, and their eyes met. Ewen's were wide, injured, unbelieving; Neil's stony, but I could see the effort that kept them level. He was hating this. So, as a matter of fact, was I. I took the woman's way out. I retreated to the scullery to fill the kettle for a cup of tea.

"All right," said Ewen to Neil. "So supposing *you* explain. When am I supposed to have broken into the house, and why on earth should you think I know anything about any of the guns?" He sat back, apparently at his ease now, and crossed his legs. He was sitting in the same chair he had had before, on that late-night chat. "Go on, Mr. Parsons. Explain."

There was a slight flush on Neil's cheekbones, and he seemed to be avoiding Ewen's eye. In view of the latter's steady, incredulous gaze, I could not blame him. He spoke to the hearthrug.

"I have already told Sergeant Fraser what
happened. I was in the house the night you
came back, and I watched you try the french
windows, and then go round to the back to
find the kitchen window locked, too. Possibly this made you uneasy, or possibly, with
the storm blowing up, you did not want to
take your boat across to the mainland again,
so you decided to let things alone, and not
risk taking any stolen goods on board. I
watched you make off along the cliff path,
as if you were making for Otters' Bay. The
lawyers had told me that the cottage was
let to a girl, who was here alone. For all I
knew she was with you, but if she was just
a visitor, I had to make sure she would be
all right. So I followed you over, and found
you here in the cottage. You had told Dr.
Fenemore that you thought your parents still
lived here. That may have been true, but for
the moment it's irrelevant."

"That's wonderful!" Ewen was letting an-
ger show now through the hurt. "Anything
that 'may be true' is irrelevant! I'll tell you
what is irrelevant, all that breaking and en-
tering bit. You've just said yourself that all I
did was try the windows. And why not? I'd
been welcome in that house for as long as

you had—longer, because you were away and I just about lived there. So go right ahead. What's all this about stolen goods and, for God's sake, guns?"

"Only that it wasn't your first visit since my great-aunt's death," said Neil. "You heard me say you 'came back.' I don't know when the first visit was, but it must have been very recent, possibly within a few days of your, er, release." He paused, and looked across at Fraser.

The sergeant nodded. "We know you hired a boat," he said, "straight away after you came out of prison, and came up to Oban. It was possible that you would come over to Moila, and of course there was nothing suspicious about that. And of course, to start with, we knew nothing about the boat's history. That, if you will allow the word, is also, for the moment, irrelevant." An explosive sound from Ewen, which was ignored. The sergeant continued: "But then Mr. Hamilton found the valuable guns missing from Taigh na Tuir, and he reported that, with the story of your attempt to get into the house last Wednesday night. So our inquiries—and possibly the search of your boat—"

"Will get you nowhere. In fact," said

Ewen—and was there just a shade of genuine relief in his tone?—"you don't know anything at all. And as for the guns that are supposed to be missing from Taigh na Tuir, I can tell you all you want to know about that. When the Colonel was alive, he always took me shooting with him, and I helped look after his guns. He had quite a few, half a dozen there in the gunroom, with the light one he got for Neil as a boy, and I used to use. Mrs. Hamilton hated guns, and never shot." He looked up at Neil. "Nor did you, when you could get out of it. And I was here when the Colonel died. You were in Australia, but even if you didn't know, the police here should have known. . . . The guns were sold. There were some that were quite valuable, a Churchill, I think, and a Boss, but they were sent to his gunsmith in Glasgow, Peterson and Briggs, and they were sold. As far as I know, the gunroom's been empty ever since. You should know, Inspector. Don't you have to check them all nowadays?"

It was Neil who answered. "You haven't mentioned the Purdeys."

"Purdeys?"

"Don't pretend you didn't know about

them. His favourite guns, the 'specials' that were made for his father in 1906, in the great days of shooting-parties. He shot once with King Edward. You knew all that, it was one of his favourite stories, and you must have known all about the guns. If they were valuable when Uncle Fergus died, they're astronomical now."

"Well, and so what about them? Of course I remember them. He would never let me touch them, always cleaned them himself. They were sold with the rest, weren't they?"

"No. They were never sold, though the lawyers thought they had gone with the others. My great-aunt may even have deceived them deliberately; I don't know. I know she would never have parted with them. Her husband had asked her to keep them for me—keep them in the family, that is, but she didn't want to be troubled with all the precautions and inspections since the Firearms Acts. In fact I'm not sure that she even attempted to understand them. She merely packed the pair of Purdeys away in a trunk in the attic, locked the trunk, and told no one, and it must have been assumed that they were sold with the rest of his things. She left a letter for me, and she did include the Purdeys in her Will, and told us where to look. I looked, yesterday, and found the trunk empty. So I went to the mainland to report it, and we have been in touch with the lawyers, the gunsmiths, and the sale-rooms. No trace, but from our description one saleroom—it was Christie's—quoted us about thirty thousand pounds."

"So?" Ewen's air was still jaunty, but the syllable came tightly.

"So it occurred to me that you, as my great-uncle's ghillie, might even have known what his plans were for his 'specials.' And putting that together with your visits to the house, and the guns' disappearance—"

Ewen had himself in hand again. He appealed to the sergeant. "Do you hear that? And you call this grounds—*grounds* for suspicion? Isn't it time you either made a charge and got it over with, or you damned well got out of here, and Mister Bloody Hamilton with you?"

The sergeant did not answer. His head was turned towards the door, where we could hear footsteps approaching. I glanced at Ewen, relaxed once more in his chair, as the door opened and one of the Customs men came in.

His eyes sought the sergeant's, and he shook his head. "Nothing. Of course it's only a rummage-search, but as far as we've gone, there's nothing in that boat at all that hasn't a right to be there."

It seemed as good a moment as any for a change of scene. I carried a tray across and set it down on the table in the window. Outside it was full daylight. Soon the sun would break through the mist. I sat down by the table and lifted the pot.

"Would anyone like a cup of tea?"

CHAPTER 16

It seemed that the cliché of the detective story—that a policeman drinks nothing when on duty—did not apply in the islands. After that sea-trip through the damp mists of early morning, I didn't blame them. The sergeant accepted a cup of tea, then gave a nod to the detective-constable which the latter seemed to understand. He took the cup I gave him over to Ewen, who accepted it politely, shook his head to the sugar-bowl, and then sat sipping, for all the world as if this were a normal tea-party and he was waiting for someone to start the conversation.

As, of course, he was. For him, so far so good. Plenty of talk, but no proof of anything but a misdemeanor, so keep quiet and let the opposition make the running. . . .

I poured tea for the four of them, then

went to refill the pot. When I had filled my
own cup and sat down again by the table,
the sergeant was speaking to Neil.

"So would you tell us, sir, what happened
tonight after you got back to Moila? You did
appear to be pursuing Mr. Mackay's boat.
Have you any reason, other than the suspi-
cions you have told us of, and Mr. Mackay's
visit to your house, when you say he did *not*
break in, for pursuing him here, and in what
looked like a dangerous manner?"

I saw Ewen smile into his tea-cup, and
spoke. "Mr. Fraser—Sergeant—may I tell
you what happened before Mr. Hamilton got
back here to Moila tonight?"

He looked surprised. "Then you were not
on the mainland with Mr. Hamilton?"

"That's right. I was not. I didn't even know
he had gone to the mainland. When I saw
his boat wasn't in the boat-house I thought
he might have gone fishing. I spent the night
on the island where the broch is." I set my
cup down. "I can't pronounce its name. The
one opposite Mr. Hamilton's house. In English it's Seal Island."

"I know the one. Eilean na Roin. Yes, Miss
Fenemore?"

The constable, Jimmy, was writing busily.

I did not look at Ewen, but was conscious that he had gone very still. I cleared my throat. "I won't make a long story of it, but I went across there after lunch, to the House. I thought I might see Mr. Hamilton there. He has told you about his first visit here; we have met since that day, and he asked me to go over whenever I wanted to. Well, I wanted to visit the island—Seal Island—because Mr. Hamilton had told me there really were seals there. I went to the house first, and he wasn't there. Then I found that the boat-house was empty, so I assumed he was away with the boat, perhaps on the island, looking at the rocks on the far side—you know he's a geologist, I suppose?—or else out fishing. Well, I went across and the seals were there and I watched them. A bit later I found that my watch had stopped, and I had misjudged the tide. When I found that I couldn't cross by the causeway I went up to Mr. Hamilton's tent and made myself some supper." I looked at Neil. "I didn't think you'd mind."

"Of course I don't. You're welcome."

"And just where is all this getting us?" asked Ewen. He set his empty cup down with a thump on the floor beside his chair, and gripped the chair-arms as if about to rise. "Sergeant Fraser, do I have to say it again? Either you will show grounds for holding me, or you will please let me go, always providing that my boat is undamaged by your pals out there, or by my friend Neil's lousy seamanship."

The sergeant ignored him. "Go on, please, Miss Fenemore."

"I was hoping that Mr. Hamilton might bring his boat in, and take me off the island, but he didn't come, so I went into the tent and went to sleep. I woke a bit later, and thought by the light that enough time might have passed for the tide to have turned. I went outside the tent, and then I heard a boat's engine. Of course I thought it would be Mr. Hamilton, so I put my jacket and shoes and things on again, and went down to the causeway. Then I saw Mr. Mackay. He must have berthed his boat in Halfway House and then come round the cliff path and down to the pier."

Dead silence. I had never had a more attentive class. The sergeant sat back in his chair. As if at a signal, the constable took over. "You're sure it was Mr. Mackay?"

"Certain. If you know the island you'll

know that the channel isn't wide, and I was at the end of the causeway and he came right down to look in the boat-house. I suppose to check that it was empty."

Ewen said sharply: "Guesswork or lies, what does it matter? Sergeant, can't you see that there's nothing here? Low tide was between quarter and half past four this morning. She was stuck on the other side till three o'clock or near it. Could you identify anyone at that hour, and in that light?"

"If I was you I'd keep quiet, sir, and let the lady finish," said the sergeant. "Go on, please, miss. Never mind what you supposed. Just tell us what you saw."

I took a deep breath. Somehow, telling my story in that charged atmosphere was like swimming against a strong current. "I saw Mr. Mackay get out some binoculars and look at the tent. I had closed it. He must have thought—sorry, skip that. Then he turned and went in through the garden gate. That path leads to the house."

"Could you see the house from where you were?" That was the sergeant.

When I said "No," he nodded, and I realized that of course he knew the house, too. I plowed on. "I waited, and after a while—I put it at about half an hour—he came back, and he was carrying a bag over his shoulder. It was about the size—it could have been a duffel bag. It seemed to be quite heavy. He left it behind the boat-house and went back to the—that is, through the garden gate again."

"Ah," said Ewen, "we have stopped supposing, have we?" The words were mocking, but when, caught off guard by the interruption, I met his eye, there was no mockery there. Anxiety, appeal, the knowledge that here, at last, was coming something that could be verified. That picture, that totally irrelevant portrait of Great-Uncle Fergus Hamilton, was still propped behind the boat-house, waiting to bear my story out, and to set the police searching for the duffel bag, which he must have dumped somewhere during the chase along the coastline. I remembered suddenly how *Stormy Petrel* had crept out of view behind the big rock stack, close inshore, presumably after Ewen had seen the Customs launch approaching. Had he dumped the bag there somewhere, to be called for later?

They say that a computer works a problem out, from given data, in milliseconds. It still has nothing on the human brain. In the micro-moment when I reluctantly met Ewen Mackay's gaze, I had gone back through all I knew of his story. The adopted boy, the good parents and their efforts to combat the bad heredity; the boredom of life on the quiet, remote island for an active, wild, and clever boy with the added qualities of looks and charm. A boy who shared, with every other normal human child, the desire to be noticed, to be someone, to be important. And to the old gentleman at the big house, the Colonel, he did become important. Neil—presumably to damp Ewen's pretensions—had used the word "ghillie"; Ewen himself had put it differently; he had been the old man's "companion" whenever he went shooting. It was possible that the boy had really liked the old man, and the Colonel seemed to have trusted him. Then the Colonel died, and the widow (could one, wise after the event, ascribe it to that legendary feminine instinct?) had found no place for him. So the boy, with possible dreams of a better "adoption" dashed, had left Moila, and, in the congenial bustle and anonymity of a big city, had learned to use the cleverness and charm and the middle-class manners he had learned, and had done well by them until some mistake was made, and he paid for it. Paid for it: and here Mrs. McDougall's words flashed up on the computer screen, to be immediately blanked out and replaced by all I had seen and heard of Ewen myself since that Wednesday night. This was exactly what he had counted on before; other people's kindness and pity were, to him, weapons to his hand. Great-Aunt Emily Hamilton was just another widow to be robbed. And for the moment it was up to me to see that he did not get away with it.

"When he came back to the boat-house," I said, "he was carrying a large picture. An oil painting. He put that in the same place, behind the boat-house. Then he grabbed the duffel bag and set off up the cliff path with it. Neil's boat came in soon after, and when we heard Ewen's engine start we went after him. The duffel bag—well, never mind, that's supposition. But the picture is still there." I drew a breath and said, not happily: "That's all."

"Well," said Ewen, "I should hope it is." He got to his feet and held out his wrists in a consciously theatrical gesture. "I give up.

I did go up to the Hamilton house this morning in the small hours, and I did take down
a picture. I admit it. But it was not theft. It
was Colonel Hamilton's portrait, and I reckoned it was due to me. The Colonel always
said I was like a son to him, the only son
he had ever had, and Mrs. Hamilton said
that when she had gone I might have it to
remember him by—"

"She would never have done that. She
disliked and distrusted you," said Neil, an-
grily.

"And what would you know about that?
You were never there. Only on holiday from
school, so what would you know about the
way they felt about me?"

"Plenty." Suddenly, between the two
men, a real spurt of antagonism had sprung
up. "And what you felt about them, too. Oh,
yes, you got on fine with my great-uncle,
but you and Aunt Emily never hit it off, and
there are plenty of folk in Moila who know
that and will swear to it."

"Then will you tell me why I should go to
the trouble and the risk, yes, because I'm
admitting I went into the house, and I did it
while you were out because I knew fine that
this was the line you'd take—why should I

want the picture, if it wasn't promised, and if it wasn't that he'd been like a father to me, more than the one I'd had to call my own?"

There it was again, the indefinable but clear emphasis on the word "father." It was clear to me because of Ewen's earlier hint at a possible connection between himself and Neil's family, the suggestion that the adopted son of the gardener might in fact be a Hamilton love-child, and hated therefore by the Colonel's wife.

"Probably," said Neil, in a tone nastier than I would have thought him capable of, "because you heard my great-aunt say that it was the most valuable thing in the house, and you're too damned ignorant to know better."

"And was it?" asked the sergeant, who, ignoring Ewen's theatrical gesture, had seemed quite content to watch and listen.

"Valuable? Heavens, no, it's very ordinary. But it was like him, and so she valued it."

Quite suddenly, I had had enough. I got to my feet.

"Sergeant Fraser, if you'll excuse me. It's been a long night, and I want a bath and a change and some breakfast. The first two right this minute. Of course you're welcome to stay as long as you have to, and if you're still here when I come down I'll see what I can manage for breakfast."

He was beginning some sort of protest about that, but I did not stay to listen. I went upstairs and into my bedroom and shut the door.

I have not yet got it straight with my subconscious. It is possible, I admit, that I deliberately wasted time in the hope that it would all be over and the police, preferably along with Ewen Mackay, would be gone before I went downstairs again. I did not know whether in fact any charge could be brought; that would surely depend on whether the duffel bag could be found, and what its contents were. The picture, except in so far as it bore my story out, could be ignored. It was even possible, I thought, as I stripped off my slept-in clothes and reached for a dressing-gown, that the whole situation would collapse into a mere incident of petty theft; it was the alleged theft of the guns that had brought the police across so quickly, and there seemed to be no way of knowing if Ewen had ever touched them.

Was it, as he had bitterly pointed out, a case of "give a dog a bad name"? It was an uncomfortable thought, but there was nothing to be done except tell the truth and leave it to the professionals. I could hear them still at it, question and answer, when I crossed the little landing to the bathroom and shut the door. Then nothing could be heard above the gushing of the taps.

Back in my bedroom, still not hurrying, I dressed. As I was brushing my hair, a sound from outside took me over to the window, to see Archie's Land-Rover starting on its careful way downhill towards the cottage. There was someone with him—two people, I thought.

I whirled to look at the bedside clock. Surely the ferry was not in yet? It was not due for another half hour at least. My brother could not get here much before nine or half past, and I had been counting on this unpleasant situation's resolving itself before that.

The Land-Rover bumped down the last curve of the track, and came to a halt. Ann Tracy jumped out, with Megan behind her. Someone must have opened the cottage door, because I heard them come right in, and then a babel of voices and questions.

It could not be put off further. I went downstairs.

CHAPTER 17

"Here she is!"

"Oh, Rose!"

Megan and Ann spoke together. They were both sitting at the table in the window. Just inside the door, which was shut, stood Archie McLaren. Seeing the boats at the jetty, he must have come with the girls to the cottage to see what was happening, and now, presumably, he would stay to see the drama out, and the ferry passengers would have to take care of themselves.

The scene in my sitting-room was certainly set for drama. Ewen still sat in the chair by the hearth, with Sergeant Fraser across from him, but the detective-constable had moved his chair to block the doorway to the scullery, and Neil was beside the fireplace, standing with an elbow on the mantelshelf. Someone had pushed the Calor gas poker into the dead logs in the fireplace, and added the rest of the peat from the hearth. The fire had caught, and was burning cheerfully.

"Hullo, there. Good morning, Archie." I greeted the newcomers a little uncertainly, then—because doing something, anything, was better than standing there trying not to look at Ewen—went to pull the gas poker out of the fire and turn it off. "An early call? Have you had breakfast?"

It was a silly remark in the circumstances, but it bridged the moment. Ann spoke breathlessly She looked tense and excited.

"Rose, we had to come. . . . Of course we didn't know anything like this had happened, the police being here, I mean, and Mr. Hamilton, but when Archie told us, we knew we'd have to come and tell you what happened yesterday."

I went across to the sofa and sat down, looking enquiringly at Sergeant Fraser.

He nodded. "Yes, it does have to do with this. It seems that while you were away on the island yesterday, the young ladies came down here. What they have told us may be important, but since you are the owner, the lessee, rather, of this cottage, we waited for you. Perhaps Miss Tracy or Miss Lloyd would repeat their story for you?"

I raised my brows at them. Megan, looking flushed and unhappy, shook her head. Ann leaned forward.

"Yes. We came down here in the evening. Yesterday evening. We wouldn't have disturbed you if you'd been busy, but we wanted to watch for the otters again. You weren't at home, so we went up there"—she gestured vaguely—"behind the cottage, and found a place we could watch from without being seen. You know, a hide."

"Ann." It was Megan, her voice low. "Not all that. Just finish."

Ann took a breath. She seemed to have no difficulty in looking at Ewen. "All right. He came. Ewen Mackay there. His boat came in to the jetty. He got out and went to the cottage door and knocked. Because of what we had heard about him, we stayed where we were and didn't say anything. He knocked again, but of course there was no answer. Then he went in. He had a key. We didn't know what to do, so we stayed put and watched. He didn't stay long—just went in and called out, as if he was checking to see that the place was empty. Then he went back to his boat." She paused. "Megan?"

"No. You."

"He took something out of the boat, a bundle. It was wrapped in what looked like cloth, thick, but it was long, and stiff, not just cloths, I mean. He went round the back to that shed, not the loo, the tool-shed, and of course that was just below us and we saw it all. He was hurrying. He went into the shed. He wasn't there long. When he came out he didn't have the bundle. He went to the boat and then away."

She stopped. Silence for a moment. Megan said, miserably: "We waited, but you didn't come, so after a bit we went down and had a look in the shed, but there wasn't anything to see. Nothing that seemed to matter, I mean. So we went home. We thought of telling Mrs. McDougall, but we decided you ought to know first. Anyway, she'd gone to bed. She leaves the door for us—actually I don't think it's ever locked. Then this morning Archie came in at break-fast-time and said the police were here, and the Customs, so we knew there must be something really wrong, and he said he'd bring us down."

The sergeant got to his feet. "You did right, miss. And now, Miss Fenemore, with your permission, we would like to take a look at that shed ourselves." A look down at Ewen. "Unless Mr. Mackay would like to save us the trouble?"

Ewen smiled at him. He had abandoned any pretense of indignation, and was merely patient and interested. "Look and be damned," he said, and leaned back in his chair.

"Very well. Jimmy, you stay here, but give a shout for Sandy to come in here, will you? . . . No, not you, Archie. There's the ferry now, did you not hear her? You'd better go. You'll hear soon enough what happens—but till you do, see you keep your mouth shut, do you mind me?"

"I mind you." Archie sketched a farewell gesture to me and the girls, and went, so quickly and willingly that I was surprised, till I remembered that of course he would be back here very soon with Crispin, and possibly in time to see the result of the search.

"Just a minute." Neil put a hand out as the detective, with one of the Customs men, made for the door in Archie's wake. "If I come with you—"

"No. You'll stay here, please, Mr. Hamilton." The sergeant did not add that three women would be no help if Jimmy should have any trouble with Ewen, but his meaning was plain enough. I expected to see Ewen smile, but saw, with a queer, unpleasant little thrill, that he was staring up at Neil, with something new in his face. He had lost colour again, and over the prison pallor shone a faint sheen of sweat, and I saw him swallow a couple of times, as if his throat hurt him.

Neil said: "I doubt if they would find anything, Sergeant, short of taking the shed to pieces, but if you let me go, I know where to look. I suppose there'd better be someone with me, as witness—"

"All right," said Ewen abruptly. "All right." He sat up, flexing his shoulders, and slanted a look up at Neil. I saw nothing there now but a sourly humorous acceptance. "I'd forgotten. Stupid of me."

"Forgotten what?" demanded the sergeant. He looked alert and vigorous, not like a man who had lost a night's sleep. At his gesture, the other men stayed where they were.

It was Neil who answered him. "Only that

he stole my trout rod once, when we were boys, and I saw him fishing with it later, and followed him back home—here—and watched him hide it in a place he'd made in the garden shed. There were a few other things there that I knew had gone missing from people's boats and gardens and so on. I didn't give him away—boys of that age don't—so his parents never knew. I waited till I saw him using the rod again, and, well, I took it back." He looked at Ewen, and for the first time there was something like sympathy there. "Eventually."

"It was quite a fight," agreed Ewen. "Well, go on. Go and get them."

"The Purdeys?"

"The Purdeys. And I hope you get well and truly done for all the years of illegal possession."

The sergeant nodded at Jimmy, and he, with Neil and one of the Customs officers, went out of the cottage.

I caught Megan's eye, and what I saw there made me get to my feet.

"Sergeant Fraser, my brother is due to arrive on this ferry, so Archie will be down here again soon. Will you want Miss Lloyd and

Miss Tracy again, or may they go back with him?"

"Surely. I know where they are staying, and we will be in touch again before they leave. Wednesday, you said, Miss Tracy?"

"Yes, that's right." Ann was on her feet, reluctantly, I thought. Megan was already making for the door.

"Then will it be all right if we wait outside?" I asked.

"Surely," he said again. He had risen from his chair when the other men went out of the room, and now he moved to open the door for us.

Megan paused on the threshold and looked back to where Ewen sat, with every appearance of ease, in the armchair by the fire. She cleared her throat, but the words came hoarsely, in a rush. "I'm sorry. I truly am. But it was the truth." She looked and sounded like an awkward and unhappy schoolgirl.

Ewen raised his head and smiled at her, a smile full of his own powerful brand of charm. He lifted one hand, and turned it over, palm up. "Of course it was. Don't give it a thought. I never had a hope anyway, did

I? Dogs with bad names . . . Goodbye, then. Enjoy your holiday."

I saw the tears start to her eyes, and said savagely under my breath: "Damn you, Ewen Mackay!" Then, with an arm round her shoulders, I urged her through the doorway and down the path to the beach.

Ann spoke quickly, fiercely. "Look, Meg, don't upset yourself. What could we do? We had to tell the police, and it's not as if there was any doubt about it, because he admitted it himself, so it's nonsense to talk about dogs with bad names. The man's a thief and a liar, we knew that from Mrs. McDougall, and you said so yourself, remember? He had it coming to him, so don't talk such balls!"

"It was a Judas thing to do. I know Mrs. McDougall told us about him, but he was nice to us, and we didn't have a thing against him ourselves. I know we had to tell the police, but it still feels like a Judas thing to do."

I sat down on the edge of the jetty, where it jutted from the sand above the high-tide mark, and pulled her down beside me.

"Megan." I was still angry, but not with her. "This is nonsense, and you've got to snap

out of it here and now. Listen to me. I had a
talk with Mrs. McDougall myself last night—
no, Saturday night. She told me more than
she told you. Ewen Mackay is not a man to
be pitied, except in that he was born without
scruple, yes, literally without a scruple of
conscience. He had every chance, loving
parents, an indulgent patron, brains, looks,
charm. All assets. The only thing he didn't
have was money, and to get that he set out
in cold blood to rob people—some of them
as poor as himself, but who had spent their
lives working, and had saved something for
their old age. He robbed them, without a second thought, of everything they had. Think
about *them.* The last one—the one he went
to prison for—was an invalid of eighty-five,
and he robbed her of something less than
three hundred pounds. All she had. Not even
as much as it would cost him to hire that boat
of his."

"'The smiler with the knife under the
cloak,' " quoted Ann.

"It doesn't matter a damn about the guns,
or whatever he had in that duffel bag," I said.
"But you see what this dog with a bad name
is like. . . . He comes out of the slammer, having seen the notice of Mrs. Hamilton's death,

hires a boat and comes straight up here to rob the dead, and perhaps—though we don't know if that bit was true—to settle again on the parents who left their home to get away from him."

Megan nodded. "Yes, I'm sorry. I do see. It was only seeing all those police, and all they wanted was to catch him, and all he could do was sit there, and it was four to one, eight to one counting us—"

"I know. It was beastly. But there was no Judas about it. Stick to that. It's over now, anyway. There they go. And it looks as if they've found the guns."

The three men were coming round the corner of the cottage. Their search in the shed had apparently been successful. The detective-constable was carrying a slim, wrapped object, and under Neil's arm was the long, gleaming shape of a shotgun.

"They have indeed," said Ann. She did not trouble to keep the satisfaction out of her voice. "And let's hope that those so-special Purdeys do the trick, and put our friend Ewen straight back where he belongs."

Megan sent her a look where a shadow of trouble still showed, but all she said was: "I suppose it was because it was guns that the police came roaring over like that?"

"I don't think so," I said. "You heard what the sergeant said—no, that was before you came down here. Once Neil reported the guns missing they would certainly come over, but normally it would be by ferry; it wouldn't be so very urgent, and anyway I doubt if there's a police boat in Oban. But Ewen made the mistake of hiring a boat cheaply from a pal on one of the outer isles, and it was a boat that was suspected of running drugs in the islands. There've been cases, but I don't know much about them. Anyway, that's what brought the Customs men roaring over, to see if Ewen Mackay was into that racket, and I suppose the police thumbed a lift with them."

"Drugs?" Megan looked horrified.

"I don't think he had anything to do with that. He was quite genuinely shocked and scared when he knew—and furious with the pal who'd flogged him the boat. His error."

"Greed," said Ann flatly. "Tried to get a boat cheaply, so brought the sheriff's posse straight in. Serve him right. If he'd had till morning he might just have made it, and he could have come back for the loot later on."

"I still can't see why he should have gone for those guns," said Megan. "With an empty house to choose from . . . What's so special about 'Purdeys'? If he'd just gone for the silver or whatever, he might have got away with it."

"Twenty or thirty thousand pounds, and going up each year," said Ann, who knew about such things. "That's how special. I'm talking about honest prices, auction prices—if you call them honest. . . . He'd get less, of course, but it still made the trip worthwhile."

"Good heavens!" said Megan, wide-eyed. The thought, unspoken, came to me again, that Megan's assets, as the daughter of a farm worker, were much the same as Ewen Mackay's. But they had got her to Cambridge on a good scholarship, and would get her very much further.

"That's what brought him back to Moila, to pick up the guns," said Ann. "And I suppose he thought that he might as well swipe some other stuff, whatever he had in that bag. But why the portrait?"

"Yes. Why?" Megan was, I was glad to see, back to her normal self. "You can't tell me he went to all that trouble for auld lang syne?"

"You heard what Neil said," I said drily. "He'd been told that it was the most valuable thing in the house, and because he knew nothing about pictures he believed it. Pictures are going even madder than guns at auction, aren't they, Ann?"

"I don't know much more about them than Ewen Mackay does, but I wouldn't give twenty-five pounds, let alone twenty-five million, for a daub of greenery yallery flowers," said Ann, and Megan laughed. It was apparently something they had argued about before. But whatever she had been going to say was never said. Two things happened almost simultaneously.

The cottage door opened, and Ewen Mackay came out, with the two detectives, and Neil behind them. Ewen wore handcuffs.

And from the curve of the track came the note of the Land-Rover, as Archie McLaren returned to the scene of the crime, bringing my brother with him.

CHAPTER 18

He brought another man as well. Climbing carefully out of the Land-Rover came a man apparently somewhere in his fifties, dressed, incongruously for the Western Isles, in a dark business suit two sizes too big for him, complete with waistcoat and a tie of such subdued and dreary colours that it had to be regimental or public school. His face, like his figure, looked as if it was meant to be fat and good-natured, but had been reduced by a very effective slimming diet, so that his cheeks looked flabby and his neck showed folds below the chin. His hair had thinned and receded, and showed a pepper-and-salt powdering of grey. With his pointed nose, smallish mouth, and twinkling eyes of some shade between grey and green, he looked like a good-tempered gnome. Of the Zürich, rather than the Disney variety: the suit was expensive, and his wrist-watch and cufflinks had the rich and unmistakable glint of gold.

In contrast my brother Crispin, tall and thin, was dressed exactly like a doctor on holiday, that is to say in old trousers only just reputable enough for the train journey, and an ancient sweater. He slid down from the Land-Rover, ignoring the offer of a helping hand from his companion, and got himself adjusted to the elbow crutch he had mentioned, a strong affair of tubular chromium which supported wrist and elbow on the injured side. His movements were careful, and he limped slightly, but he walked well enough to meet me, and leaned down to kiss my cheek.

"Rose. You look wonderful, and what a great place you've picked." He did not appear to have noticed anything strange, yet, about the group of men further down the beach at the boats. "This is Hartley Bagshaw, who travelled up with me."

"Mr. Bagshaw," I said, and shook hands, murmuring the usual things about hoping the journey had been comfortable, and had they had breakfast, while wondering madly why Crispin had brought him along, and was I going to have to put him up and feed him, and at the same time trying not to miss what was going on down at the jetty's end. "Are you on holiday, too?"

But Mr. Bagshaw's gaze had gone past me, and he certainly had not missed what was going on. "What the hell?" he said, explosively. "That's a police boat, isn't it?"

"No, Customs, but—"

"And those men—they've got to be policemen. They *are* policemen! What goes on?" And then, fortissimo, "Ewen Mackay? *Ewen Mackay?*"

The police had looked our way as the Land-Rover stopped, then had made some sort of tactful haste to get their man away before my visitors arrived. But now the whole group froze as Ewen, in the act of stepping, escorted, into the launch, stopped and turned, with the handcuffs clearly visible.

Mr. Bagshaw froze, too, for two long seconds; then, starting forward, he exploded again into speech, and I learned three new words in the next three seconds, and then several interesting ways of using well-known and respectable words that would never have occurred to me in a lifetime. I caught a glimpse of Archie's face of startled horror, of Ann's mouth dropping open, of Megan's flushed cheeks; then Sergeant Fraser barked something, Ewen held up his cuffed wrists and laughed, and Mr. Bagshaw shut his mouth with a snap, said: "I beg your pardon, ladies. I got a shock. The police seem to have arrested a friend of mine. It must be a mistake. Excuse me." And he darted down the beach towards the group there. In spite of the apology, he was still flushed, and all the good nature had vanished from his eyes, which were bright with fury and what might have been fear. Crispin said "Steady on!" and moved to hold him back, but his injury checked him, and he stumbled, saved himself by grabbing at me, said "Damn and blast," and stood still, rubbing his leg. Archie, still looking outraged, called out: "Hey, there!" and started down the beach after Mr. Bagshaw.

It was reaction, I suppose, from the sleepless night, the unpleasant tensions of the recent interview in the cottage, and now this totally unexpected irruption into the scene. I wanted to laugh, and saw, suddenly, that the girls, clinging together on the jetty, were about to succumb to the same near-hysteria. I beckoned to them, controlling myself sharply, and when they came, introduced my brother.

"Ann, Megan, this is my brother. Crispin, meet Ann Tracy and Megan Lloyd."

That did it. If I had hoped that the semiformal introduction would sober us up, I had not reckoned on my voice sounding exactly like the lecturer's voice Megan had so wickedly imitated on the broch island; and now it was accompanied, in a cruel counterpoint, by another spate of angry and idiomatic speech from Mr. Bagshaw, every word of which carried clearly up the beach to where we stood. The girls did manage to take Crispin's hand and say something, then they both went off, helplessly, into peals of laughter.

"His friend, he said . . ." That was Ann, wiping her eyes. "What d'you suppose he calls people he doesn't like?"

"If we stay a bit longer," quavered Megan, "we might learn."

"I would like," said Crispin, "to know just what has been going on here? If you three idiots will stop laughing for a moment and tell me—"

"Idiots, he called us," wailed Ann. "So rude. And we've only just met. Oh, R-Rose—"

I took hold of myself, and of Crispin's arm. "Come on, let's go in and get ourselves some coffee. Cris, I suppose you had breakfast on the boat? Well, I haven't had mine, and I don't suppose the girls have either. I haven't a clue what's going on now, but we can talk in the house. Come on."

"They're coming back," said Megan.

She was at the window, opposite me where I sat at the table finishing my coffee. All four of us—myself, Crispin, and the girls—had started by declaring that we could not possibly eat any breakfast, and we had all ended up at the. table with mugs of coffee and a stack of toast and marmalade, with a jar of local honey on the side. Crispin had even produced a bag of fresh doughnuts which he had bought on the ferry, but we did jib at those, and put them aside "for afters." No one said "After what?" but we all knew. There would be no peace on this peaceful island until its storm center had been removed.

Which might be at any moment now. *Sea Otter* was still at the jetty, rubbing shoulders with *Stormy Petrel,* but the Customs launch had gone, not back to the mainland, but along the coast towards Halfway House and the broch island. The detective-constable had gone with it, and Neil, along with Ewen and the Customs officers. It was to be assumed that they had gone to look for the dumped duffel bag: I wondered if, having admitted to the major theft of the guns, and with the picture sitting behind the boathouse as witness of my story, Ewen would settle for cooperation as the most sensible course.

If so, they might not be gone long. It seemed that Mr. Bagshaw was nursing the same hope; he was down at the jetty, talking volubly to an impassive Sergeant Fraser, with Archie McLaren as an apparently fascinated listener. I had hoped that the latter was waiting to take Hartley Bagshaw back with him, but from what Crispin had told us, it seemed that he was here on business, and had come to see Neil.

Over our non-breakfast we had exchanged news and stories. First of all, Crispin's injury: this was still painful, but mending normally, and though it would inconvenience him for some time, would not stop him from getting around reasonably well, and the elbow crutch would allow him, he said, to use both hands for his camera. That being disposed of, we all—the girls and I—clamoured for an account of Mr. Bagshaw, but Crispin refused to speak until we had filled him in on what Ann called the Great Moila Mystery, and the girls, who of course knew very little of what had been going on, supported him, so I told my story, and afterwards answered the questions they asked, while we drank coffee and munched toast, and watched the window for the return of the launch.

"More coffee?" asked Ann, when question and answer ran at length to a standstill.

We all refused, and Megan, picking the pot up, looked a question at me. "What about Archie and Mr. Bagshaw? Shall I make some more for them?"

"Not until we've heard my brother's side of it. Cris, who is Mr. Bagshaw, what is he? And did he tell you what he wanted with Neil Hamilton?"

"And there did seem to be some connection between him and Ewen Mackay," said Megan, reaching absently for a doughnut. "Wouldn't you say?"

"They were friends, he said so," said Ann, on a little bubble of laughter. "But somehow not very likely ones. I wonder where they met?"

"I can guess," I said, and Crispin cocked an eye at me. "Am I right? Prison? Or didn't he confide in you that far?"

"Yes, it was, and oddly enough he did. There's something about coming through a disaster together that seems to lower the barriers, and he knew I was a doctor, of course. People get used to talking to us. He made no secret of the prison bit, in fact he seemed to want to go public on what had happened to him, so I'm not betraying a confidence. We travelled up together, and he did quite a lot of talking. He had just come out after doing two years, though he'd been innocent, he said, of any part in the fraud."

"Of course. But—fraud? Do you mean he was in Ewen Mackay's beastly racket, watching the obit columns and robbing lonely old women?"

"No, no. He was one of the men caught up in the Prescott take-over scandal. You remember it? Three or four years ago."

"I can't say I do. I don't take much interest

in City goings-on. Do you remember it?" This to the girls, who shook their heads.

"It doesn't matter," said Crispin. "Actually, I may say, I believe him. He told me a good deal about the Prescott affair, and when I said he was 'caught up' in it I meant just that. He's a tough little chap, self-made, from a rough background—you can ignore the Guards tie—but I'm sure he's relatively honest, and it was partly bad luck and partly a rotten partner that landed him with a conviction. However. The point is—the reason he's here—he's a property developer, and when Ewen Mackay, who was due out at about the same time, told him that he knew Moila, and that an old lady had died there recently, and there might be a good property for sale, Bagshaw was interested, and apparently Mackay promised, for a cut, of course, to help him negotiate with the family. Made out that he was practically one of them himself." He raised a brow at me.

I shook my head. "No connection," I said, "and there's no family to negotiate with, apart from Neil, who doesn't need any persuading anyway. But it figures. Ewen had plans of his own, didn't he? Go on."

"Well, from what you've just told me, I

gather that poor little Bagshaw was lined up as a victim even before Mackay got out of jail. Bagshaw arranged for Mackay to have funds to hire a boat and get up here to start things moving with the family . . . Which he certainly seems to have done."

Megan said, forcibly for her: "You were right, Rose. Not Judas stuff at all . . . Do you see? It means that even when he was in jail he was watching the papers for someone else to cheat!"

"Leopards," said Ann, "probably wouldn't change their spots even if they could."

"I wonder how much Mr. Bagshaw gave him for the boat hire?" said Megan. "And he even tried to make something out of that by taking the poor old *Stormy Petrel.*"

"His mistake," said Ann. "Go on, Crispin. So that's Mr. Bagshaw's business with Neil Hamilton? He's going to buy the house?"

"And Seal Island?" asked Megan, and looked distressed when my brother nodded.

"He's already made an offer," I told them. "At least, I suppose it was he. Through an agent. He must have set it in motion on Ewen's say-so while he was still in jail." I told them what Neil had said.

Crispin nodded again. "Yes, it was Bag-shaw. He's very keen. Apparently Mackay really sold him on it. I doubt if the house matters; he'd want something a good deal bigger, but of course there's plenty of room to build. It's the beaches and the island that are the attractions; you know the sort of thing, a marina and what he calls a big 'lei-sure center,' and a 'luxury apartment block' with a golf course—"

"Along the machair?" asked Megan, al-most in a whisper.

"If that's what it's called. The strip along the west coast. He showed me the map when we talked in the train. I did try to say something about the beauty of the islands and what this kind of development does to it, but it was no use. I know. It's grim. But what can one do?"

"Surely, there must be something?" I said. "I know Neil's thinking of selling, and in fact he's granted the option, but I doubt if he'd want to see that kind of development here, and there might just be some way to stop it, and wait for a different offer?"

"From what you've told us, I doubt it," said my brother. "Bagshaw told me about the option, and I gather he's paying a very good price—more than this sort of property usually fetches nowadays. I've no idea how binding the agreement is, or what the details are, but as I said, he's still very keen. That's all I know."

"But if Mr. Bagshaw's fury at Ewen Mackay was because Ewen had come up here on his own and couldn't resist a spot of easy pillage, perhaps he—Mr. Bagshaw—is afraid that may have queered his pitch? It sounds as if it may not be all that binding," I said hopefully. "I mean, if Ewen's a crook, and he's had something to do with the offer Mr. Bagshaw made—"

"We'll soon know," said Megan, at the window. "They're coming back."

I am not sure what I had expected to happen when the launch returned, but it was a relief to find that we were not to be confronted again with Ewen Mackay He did not, in fact, reappear, but must have been below with the detective-constable. The launch came round neatly and reversed in beside *Sea Otter*, stern to the jetty, and Neil got out; then he and the sergeant made for the cottage.

Not before, predictably, they had been

ambushed by Mr. Bagshaw, who still apparently had a great deal to say, but the sergeant forged placidly through it, and came
on up, with Bagshaw close beside him and
still talking. Neil stopped for a few moments'
chat with Archie; then he, too, came up.

The sergeant was brief. The duffel bag had
been recovered, he told us, and found to be
full of small stuff, mostly silver, but with a few
pieces of china and other objects of virtu
wrapped in towels and various kitchen
cloths, and the clock from the drawing-room
mantelpiece. Apart from one vase, which
was cracked, and the clock, which would
never be the same again, nothing was damaged. The bag had been dumped into shallow water when Ewen's boat had slipped out
of sight behind the rock stack, and had sunk
gently to lie on a sandy bottom. And yes,
they had found the portrait of Great-Uncle
Fergus, propped just as I had said behind
the boat-house, and yes, Mr. Mackay had
been helpful in the recovery of the duffel bag,
and would now go back to the mainland to
assist the police with their inquiries. . . . And
no, there was no need for any further search
of *Stormy Petrel.* They were satisfied that Mr.
Mackay had nothing to do with any Customs

offense, so the boat could remain here. He understood that Mr. Bagshaw had in fact provided the money for the hire, so if he wished to use the boat he was free to do so.

Meanwhile, said Sergeant Fraser, suddenly human, he was sorry to have had to intrude on Miss Fenemore's holiday, and he hoped there would be no further trouble. Of course Mr.—or was it Professor?—Hamilton would have to be called upon later, and statements would be taken from Miss Fenemore and the young ladies, but in the meantime he hoped that we would forget all about it and enjoy our holiday, and now he really must go. . . .

I shook hands with him and murmured something, conscious again of that missed night's sleep, and of quite a lot of talking to get through before peace came back to the ivory tower. But, mercifully, Mr. Bagshaw seemed content to keep quiet and let the sergeant go. From the fragments of speech I had overheard as the men came up to the cottage, I thought that he, Mr. Bagshaw, had been eagerly trying to dissociate himself from Ewen Mackay's latest exploits, except as the innocent provider of *Stormy Petrel,* and was now only anxious to be allowed to sink into the background and see the Customs launch safely on its way.

Finally the sergeant took himself off. Neil went with him down to the jetty, stood for a few moments more talking, then the two men shook hands, and the policeman jumped aboard. The launch moved off, took a gentle curve out of the little bay, then, with a suddenly white wake, headed fast for open water and was lost to sight beyond the headland.

It was as if its disappearance had been a signal, as definite as the dropping of the curtain in a play. Drama and mystery were finished with; here was only a group of ordinary people who wanted to get on with their ordinary lives; who had been touched for a moment with the end of a live wire and shocked into unaccustomed and unpleasant action, then left to recover themselves and hope for the burns to heal.

Archie, with a muttered word, went down to the Land-Rover and lugged Crispin's cases out of the back. Crispin, limping after him, lifted out the precious camera equipment himself. They took the things upstairs and into the bedroom I showed them. Megan was busily clearing the table, and

Ann had vanished into the scullery, from which presently came the sound of washing-up and the smell of fresh coffee brewing. Mr. Bagshaw, silent now and looking exhausted, had sunk into the chair recently vacated by Ewen Mackay, and was staring at the ashes of the fire. In the wrinkled clothes that had fitted him before the years in prison, he looked deflated and absurd, and, somehow, suddenly vulnerable.

I said gently: "Mr. Bagshaw, you must be tired. There'll be some coffee in a minute, and then perhaps you'll let Archie McLaren take you back to the village. Why not leave your business with Mr. Hamilton till after you've rested? I'm sorry we haven't room to put you up here, but I'm sure Mrs. McDougall at the post office will be able to help you, or tell you where to go."

He raised his head, but did not take his eyes from the fireplace. It was as if he was speaking to the dying fire. "I had no idea he had this in mind. No idea at all. They have got to believe me."

"They do. I'm sure they do. If they hadn't believed you, they wouldn't have gone away without you, would they? They don't even think Ewen Mackay was involved in the drug thing, either, or they'd have taken the boat for a detailed search. You heard them say so. What's been happening here isn't any-thing to do with you at all."

His eyes came to me then. "I couldn't go back there, Miss Fenemore. I told your brother about it. We came up together in the train. I told him about it then."

"Yes, I know."

"He saved me, you know. We were in that train accident together, the one that came off the rails near Kendal. When the engine went off the line, and the crash came, I was caught under something, I couldn't see what, it was so dark, but he pulled me out. Your brother pulled me out."

"Did he? I didn't know that. It must have been awful. Were you hurt?"

"No, no. Bruises and shock, that's all. But if he hadn't pulled me out . . . Just after he did it, the whole thing slid down the bank and I might have been killed. That's when his foot was hurt, but even after that he was trying to help some of the people."

"Yes, well, he's a doctor. They do."

"Then when we were taken to hospital we found we were both coming up here to Moila, so I said I'd wait a couple of days, to be in the train with him, you see, in case he needed looking after. Carrying luggage and all that. So when they let him out of hospital he took me with him to stay with his friends in Glasgow. They were very kind. Both doctors, he's a heart surgeon and she—Laura—she's a pediatrician. But I forgot, you probably know them. Anyway, I stayed there, and then came up with him. It was the least I could do."

"It was good of you. I'm sure it was a help."

"But don't you see—" He sat up as he spoke, and with the bitter spice in his voice, the life had come back to it. The dull eyes began to brighten. "But don't you see, if I had come straight up here—and I could have got the Saturday's boat—I could have stopped that f—pardon, I'm sure—that stupid, bloody, sorry, Mackay from taking all that stuff and bringing the police down on our necks when all this is above-board and a perfectly straight transaction, because whatever was said at the time, and your brother knows all about this because we talked it over as I told you, I did not know what was going on, or I do assure you I'd have been out from under, because I didn't get much out of it all except a couple of years that I'd sooner forget, and don't intend ever to repeat, and if I had known what that Mackay intended, do you suppose I'd have left him up here on his own to queer my pitch and make a—a mess like this?"

"Coffee?" said Ann, from the doorway. She came in with a tray, and crossed to the table. "Milk and sugar, Mr. Bagshaw?"

"Yes. Thanks. Both, thanks."

"And a doughnut?" asked Megan, coming in with a plate. "They're terrific. If I wasn't a student of Dr. Fenemore's and a fan of Hugh Templar's I'd say *fantastic.*" She met my eye. "Yes, I'm sorry, Rose, but you did leave your papers there on the window-sill, and I honestly couldn't help seeing. I say it again. Lit. and met., fantastic."

"What are you talking about?" Ann, spooning out sugar for Mr. Bagshaw, did not sound interested. "Oh, Archie, there you are. Coffee?"

"Thanks, I don't mind." Archie came down the stairs and took a mug. "Just a half, though. I'd best be getting away again. Thanks. You'll be coming with me, ladies? And you?" This to Mr. Bagshaw, who gave me a glance and then nodded.

"I guess so. I guess you're right, my dear.

I'll not impose on you any longer. You look tired, and I reckon nothing good will come of this day until we've all rested and got ourselves back to normal. Mr. Hamilton's still out there, is he? I'll get a time fixed with him, and maybe we'll meet again later. You've been very kind, and I'll call on your brother again before I go back to London." He heaved himself to his feet and put his mug down on the table. "And when I get the place going here— and your brother will tell you the plans I've got—you and he will always be welcome, and I'll personally see you get the best of everything Moila has to offer."

"Thank you very much."

He held out a hand and I took it. "Give my best to your brother, and I hope that foot will soon be better." In the doorway a thought seemed to strike him, and he paused. "That boat, now. It looks as if I'm stuck with that boat, and I wouldn't know how to handle it, not in this sort of place. If you and your brother would like the use of it—nothing to pay, of course, it's all seen to—you're very welcome, and when you're finished with it, just leave it; I can find some way of getting it picked up and taken back where it came from. With your brother lame as he is, a boat might be a good way of getting around to see places."

"Well, how very good of you." It would have seemed ungracious to say that I was counting on the use of Neil's boat, with Neil to manage it, so I merely thanked Mr. Bagshaw again and watched while he made his way down to where Neil, in *Sea Otter,* was busy with the engine hatch open. The two of them spoke briefly, and I saw Neil pointing in the direction of Taigh na Tuir, and then Mr. Bagshaw shook hands with him, too, and climbed into the Land-Rover. It moved off up the hill.

The girls came out of the scullery.

"Don't worry," said Ann, "we're going. Let you and your brother say hello to each other and have a bit of peace. You look as if a long sleep wouldn't come amiss, either. Come on, Meg."

"But Archie's just gone," I said.

"I know. We told him we'd walk back. Believe it or not, the day's yet young, and we've got a picnic here. We thought we'd go back along the machair."

"While it's still there," said Megan. "Before the golf balls start to fly. Do you think it would be safe to have a swim?"

"I don't know. Ask Neil."

"I didn't mean currents and things. I meant swim raw. We haven't got swimsuits."

"Oh. I still don't know, but good luck to it. It's a gorgeous day for it. Well, thanks for all your help. Come back, won't you, when ever you want to?"

"Love to," they said. "Goodbye."

As they set off Megan looked back over her shoulder, and said, under her breath: "Fantastic!"

"What?" asked Ann.

"Nothing," said Megan. "A rose by any other name. Come on."

They picked their way down to where Neil still stooped over *Sea Otter.* There was a brief conversation, then Neil jumped out onto the pier and came up to the cottage, while the girls waited.

He looked in at the cottage door. "Rose. Are you all right? It's been a grim morning for you."

"For us all. Yes, thank you, I'm fine. What happens now?"

"Now, today, nothing. They'll let me know. So try to forget it, and have a rest. I'm going back to Taigh na Tuir, and I'm taking the girls

round in the boat; it'll give them a short cut
to the machair. So I'll be off now."

"You are coming over for supper tonight,
aren't you? We'd love to have you."

"I'd like that very much. If you're sure—"

"Of course. I'll do nothing all day, and
Crispin's brought some goodies, so the
meal's no problem. And there's still a lot I
want to ask you before I can really start to
forget it all."

"Then I'll come with pleasure. About
seven?"

"Yes. And—Neil."

"Yes."

"It's none of my business, but has Mr.
Bagshaw said anything yet about the
House? The sale, I mean?"

"No. We've arranged to meet there tomorrow, and I'll show him round. But let's
forget that, too, for the present, shall we?
Tonight at seven, then. Goodbye."

CHAPTER 19

It was after supper that evening. After its explosive start, the day had been peaceful. No one had called at the cottage. I had caught up on some of the sleep I had missed, and then through a long day of sunshine and soft breezes Crispin and I had talked, and lazed, and talked again, till we had caught up on our personal news, and I had told him all I knew about the recent happenings on Moila. Supper was easy, cold chicken and ham with salad, followed by the promised strawberries, and some cheese brought that morning by my brother, and afterwards Neil brought out some camp chairs he had seen that morning in the shed, and set them in the grass by the cottage door. We took coffee cups out and sat there, while below us the sea creamed up over the stones of the beach, and at the jetty *Sea Otter* bobbed and swayed alongside *Stormy Petrel.*

"It was rather sweet of him." I had been telling them of Mr. Bagshaw's offer of his boat. "But I wouldn't know how to deal with it, and I'm not sure if Cris could either. Could you?"

"I could try," said my brother. "If Neil will give me a couple of driving lessons, and if I don't have to use this foot of mine. A boat could come in very handy."

Neil laughed. "The driving part couldn't be simpler, but I'm afraid you'd have to be a bit more active than you think. There's a lot of clambering about to be done, and even getting in and out of the dinghy would be a problem for you for the next few days. No, you'd better forget *Stormy Petrel,* at any rate for now, and until Archie and I have had time to go over her for damage. I saw a couple of nasty-looking scrapes that look fresh. Ewen must have squeezed it a bit, to get right into the shallows behind that stack. Meantime there's my boat, and I'll be very happy to take you both wherever you want to go."

"Well, thank you," said Crispin. "That sounds to me an altogether better idea."

"Once I've got tomorrow over, that is." Neil set his cup down on the grass beside his chair. "I told Rose, I've arranged to see Bagshaw at the house. I'm not sure how long he plans to stay in Moila, but naturally he wants to see all there is. And as far as I'm concerned, if it has to be done, the sooner the better."

" 'If it has to be done?' Does that mean that you're changing your mind about it?"

"I don't know," said Neil heavily. He sounded tired and despondent. I had put it down to the recent happenings, which of course had been a good deal more unpleasant for Neil than for me, but now I could see that it went deeper. He looked at Crispin. "After what you've told us about his plans, he's certainly not the buyer I would have wanted, but it looks now as if that's up to him. We can only hope the place doesn't meet his standards."

"It's a problem," agreed my brother. "You might have considered handing the house to an agent for winter lets, and using it yourself in summer, but if you're teaching in Australia that's hardly feasible. I don't really see what else you can do but sell."

"My job in Sydney is finished. I'll be in Cambridge next year. So your solution, Crispin, might be possible, if only this option business can be got round."

"What changed your mind?" I asked him.

There was a silence, which all at once seemed charged, and stretched itself almost to breaking before he spoke.

"You," he said.

I stared at him.

"The way you talked at supper. The things you said about the place, the broch, the machair, this little cove with the otters. And Eilean na Roin . . . I've known all my life about the seals and the birds, and I believe I knew about the storm petrels, though I never saw one, but you talked about them"—he hesitated—"well, you talked as if the place belonged to them, and when you come to think about it, I suppose it does. I was only a boy when I was here before, and I'd forgotten. . . . Then, coming back, and going round the place with you . . ." He paused again, then added, almost as if it were something he was ashamed of admitting: "When you told us about your night on the island, and the petrels, I could see that they had really got to you. It was like, well, I suppose poets must feel that way."

I said nothing. I saw Crispin smile.

"So when I heard what Crispin had to tell us about Bagshaw's plans—Bagshaw was pretty specific, wasn't he, during that night in the train?—I knew I had to get out of the sale if I could. But how?"

"Hope that he finds the house depressing," said Crispin. "Hope that it pours tomorrow and the roof leaks and then tell him that one can never get workmen to do anything in the West Highlands. Everything's *mañana,* or whatever that is in Gaelic."

Neil laughed. "There's no such word in Gaelic. It conveys too much urgency. Any other ideas?"

"Invite him to stay," I offered, "and give him a horrible supper, and tell him that you simply cannot get supplies here in Moila, and that the electricity fails almost every night."

"The absurd thing is," said my brother, slowly, "that I rather like him. I know he's brash and full of ideas that we might find hideous, but he's not a bad sort of chap, and he's had a horrific couple of years in

jail, and I honestly believe him when he says
he got in too deep before he quite knew
what was happening. I'm talking about the
Prescott fraud case. It's just possible—no,
no, I'm talking nonsense."

"You're not. I like him myself. Go on," said
Neil.

"In the first place—I know nothing about
Scots law, but it's possible that this option
business is not binding on you, in which
case you have no problem, except what to
do with the place in the long run. But it does
occur to me that if you show Mr. Bagshaw
everything—I mean the beauties of the
place just as it is, with the birds and seals
and the machair flowers—and try to show
him how the holiday crowds would destroy
the very things that they thought they were
paying for . . . Isn't it just possible that he
might decide to go somewhere a little more
suitable?"

"It's possible, but I wouldn't bet on it,"
said Neil. "I have a feeling that the whole
setup is too tempting. We'll just have to trust
that the option won't hold water, and let me
worry about the future once Bagshaw has
given up and gone home. I won't pretend it
isn't a worry. That house won't be easy to

get rid of reasonably, even letting it as you suggested. Of course, the setting's lovely. That's what will do it, if anything does . . . You sound as if you know it. Have you been here before?"

"No. Rose has told me about it. She was, well, poetic on the subject. I can hardly wait to see the petrels. I suppose that must wait till tomorrow night, and then, if their fate is sealed, it will be a sad sort of pilgrimage."

"It needn't wait," said Neil. "We could go now, if you're not tired? You spent last night in the train, after all. And don't worry about the leg. We'll take the boat; the tide's wrong for the crossing, and in any case I'm sure you couldn't manage the causeway. You'd really like to go? What about you, Rose?"

"I've rested today. I'm fine. I'd love to go."

"Then let's do it at once," said Neil, rising. "And I doubt if there's a word in Gaelic for that, either."

They were there. There was no sound from the seals' rocks, and from the sea-birds only the occasional muted cry, sounding distant and sleepy. But the petrels were there, waiting for night. Dusk fell slowly, the veils of evening. For some time, as we sat in silence outside Neil's tent, we heard nothing but the slow hush of the sea below us, and the faint stirring of the long grasses in the dying breeze. Then at last the song began.

In that long, quiet twilight the sound was still as weird, as romantic, as spirit-stirring as anything I had ever known. We sat quite still. Nobody spoke. And then the flight began. The motes of shadow whirled and dipped, and now and again a bird went by so closely, and in such a silence of small velvet wings, that it was as if a flake of the very darkness had broken away to be blown, weightless, out to sea.

All at once, the spell was broken. Neil got to his feet suddenly, as if impelled by springs, said "Hell!" and started rubbing a hand violently over his face and hair. Then he turned and dived back into the tent, and we could hear him rummaging there.

I came back from Cloud Nine to feel my face and hands stinging and my hair itching as if I had been beaten with nettles. As the breeze had died, the midges had come out, and in force. The bracken near us would be full of them, and possibly, even, the petrels as they crept from their burrows had disturbed them and sent them to fill the air like stinging dust.

My brother, moving more clumsily and rather more slowly, was on his feet propped by the elbow crutch, and he, too, was rubbing and slapping furiously. Neil crawled out of the tent with a small plastic bottle clutched in his hand.

"Here. Shoo them," he said.

"I'm trying, but they don't take a damned bit of notice," said Crispin testily.

I laughed. "It's the name of the midge-repellent, you nit. Quick. Put it on."

"After you. Look, Rose, Neil—this has been very wonderful, and I wouldn't have missed it for worlds, but do you mind very much if we go away now, this moment, and come back another day when there's a Force Five gale?"

I handed him the bottle. "Suits me. I should have warned you. This time of year, whenever the breeze drops, the Defenders of the Highlands are out in force. Neil? You ready to go?"

"Not quite," said Neil. He finished shutting the tent, and turned to take three long paces over to where I stood waiting to help my brother down the slope.

"Excuse me," he said, and pulled me into his arms and planted a kiss on each cheek. "There. That's by way of a 'thank you.' You've just shown me what to do tomorrow. And now let's just get the hell out of this infested isle, and leave the petrels in peace."

CHAPTER 20

"I'll be frank with you," said Mr. Bagshaw, sounding very frank indeed, "there'll be a lot of work involved, and you say it's difficult to get construction work done here?"

"Almost impossible," said Neil.

"But given the time and the capital, it can be done? A good team in from Glasgow, get a supply chain going, they live in the house while they get set up, then Portakabins on that flat field by the beach . . . It could be done."

"The weather can be a problem," said Neil.

We were standing in the belvedere, which commanded a view to northward of the machair, and straight across the channel to the island where, in the sunlight, the outlines of the broch showed sharply. Down to our

left Neil's boat lay by the jetty, with Crispin
sitting in the stern, fishing.

It had been a long day. Neil had brought
Sea Otter round soon after breakfast, and
taken Crispin and me to the house. Not long
after that, Archie's Land-Rover brought Mr.
Bagshaw down, and the tour of inspection
began. At Neil's request I had stayed with
the two men while they looked over the
house, and then had—this at my own suggestion—given them lunch of a kind in the
kitchen. I had made sandwiches earlier with
the rest of the cold chicken and some ham,
and brought some cheese and fruit to finish
with. Crispin had taken his share earlier, and
had gone off on his own to look at the
machair; he had insisted that he could manage perfectly well with the elbow crutch, and
since he could obviously look after himself
we had let him go, and turned our attention
to a hopeful discouragement of Mr. Bagshaw.

It did not appear to be working. On that
lovely sunny day the house failed to look
depressing, or even very neglected, though
I drew Neil's attention twice to damp-marks
on the ceilings, and Neil responded with a
rueful remark about the state of the roof,

then checked himself with a quick, worried look at Mr. Bagshaw. The rather awful back premises of the house drew nothing more from the latter than pursed lips and a reference to the excellent architect who was, apparently, living only to make Mr. Bagshaw's dreams come true. And the weedy garden was no problem at all: with those bushes, whatever they were called, said Mr. Bagshaw, eyeing the rhododendrons with enthusiasm, all you needed to do was keep the grass cut, and who needed a garden when you had a view like this?

And of course the machair decided it. It looked, to Neil's and my fury, exactly like the most idyllic picture postcard of an island view. There was the long, gentle curve of milk-white sand, backed by a sea of turquoise and pale jade and indigo. There were the far cliffs, violet-shadowed as any classical landscape. And for the four miles of the flat coastline, between the white beach and the green slope of the moor, stretched the wild-flower meadow that in Gaelic is the machair. The turf is barely visible, starred with the tiny yellow and white flowers of tormentil and daisy and silverweed. Then comes the next layer, at a few inches high, eyebright and bugle and yellow rattle, and over these, in soft motion always in the breezes, the dog-daisies and ragwort and knapweed and brilliant hawkears and the lace of pignut and wild chervil, and the sweet delicate harebells that are the blue-bells of Scotland.

They may not all have been flowering at once, but that is the impression the machair gives you, and the scent, mingled somehow with the smell of the sea and the tangle at the tide's edge, is the unforgettable, unfor-gotten smell of the summer isles.

Mr. Bagshaw, predictably, was in ecsta-sies. The bathing, the sun-beaches, the pic-tures in the brochures, the water-sports, and yes, he supposed there were wet days, but he had been assured in the village that the television reception was OK, and in fact had watched it last night, and of course there would be the night life, the leisure center, discos . . .

So at length we came back to the garden and the belvedere. Mr. Bagshaw did not no-tice Echo and Narcissus watching us sadly from their weedy beds, or I am sure they would have inspired him to new plans, but he kept his eyes fixed on the bright prospect

framed by the trees at the end of the belvedere.

"That's the remains of a broch you can
see," said Neil. He sounded tired and dis-
pirited. "An Iron Age stronghold. You
wouldn't be allowed to touch that, of
course."

"Of course not. But it would make another attraction. Culture," said Mr. Bagshaw.
"And that's another good beach on the
other side. There's something romantic
about an island, I always think. Don't you?"

"Oh, yes. But the tides are difficult, and
the channel can be very dangerous."

Mr. Bagshaw was silent for a minute, then
turned those bright shrewd little eyes on
him. "I get the impression that you're not all
that willing to sell. Am I right?"

Neil hesitated. "I suppose so. I realize that
I may have to, but it's—well, it's not easy to
envisage such, er, changes to a place one
has known and loved. And what you pro-
pose, Mr. Bagshaw, would change the
whole island. I wouldn't want to feel respon-
sible—I mean, I did try to explain—"

"Yes, you did. But the whole world
changes, every day," said Mr. Bagshaw, with
truth, "and this sort of place has to change

with the times. People have leisure, and they want clean air and the sea, and to have fun, and if we can provide it here in this country, it keeps their cash here, doesn't it?"

"So you really want to take up the option?"

"I can see nothing against it."

"Well, that's it, then." Neil got up from where he had been sitting on the wall. "But would you like to see the little island, too? I'll take you right round it, to the bird cliffs, and then if you like we can land you to look at that beach, and the broch."

Mr. Bagshaw would be delighted. And presently he was in *Sea Otter* with the three of us and we were cruising round the outside of Eilean na Roin. The birds rose in screaming clouds, to the pleasure, different in either case, of Crispin and Mr. Bagshaw, as Neil took the boat gently on and along the machair as far as the peregrine cliffs. Then, slowly, back again. It was difficult to talk above the noise of the engine, and Mr. Bagshaw seemed deep in his own thoughts. I handed round plastic mugs of thermos tea, and then sat enjoying the colours of the advancing twilight, and the pleasure in my brother's face.

Some time around half past six the wind died, and with it the last brightness fell from the day. The evening was still far from dark, but all through the afternoon the slow clouds had been building up in the west, and as the sun sank lower behind them, twilight dimmed the outlines of the land and greyed the sea.

I saw Neil looking around him with satisfaction, and then the engine's noise sank to a mutter, and he brought the boat softly in to the inner shore of Eilean na Roin, and let her drift alongside the causeway. He jumped out and handed Mr. Bagshaw ashore.

I made ready to get out, but he shook his head at me. "Wait a bit, do you mind?" Then, to Mr. Bagshaw: "Why don't you go ahead and take a look around before it gets too dark? Take your time. I'm going over to the boat-house for a few minutes to fix something. OK?"

Mr. Bagshaw was understood to say OK, and *Sea Otter* drifted back into mid-channel. We saw Mr. Bagshaw making his way rapidly uphill towards the broch; then Neil turned the boat and headed, not for the boat-house, but for the headland beyond which lay the cove called Halfway House.

It was a narrow cove, with a wedge of stony beach, and to either side sheer-sided rocks where a boat could lie as if at a jetty. Landing was simple. We tied up to a ring that he himself, said Neil, had driven into a crevice in the rock many years ago, and silence came back as the engine died.

"Am I to understand," said Crispin, "that you are leaving the Defenders of the Highlands to do the job for you?"

"To make a suggestion merely," said Neil.

"They're making it here," I said, slapping. "Where's the stuff?"

"Some in the cabin. I never move without it."

"One sees why." Crispin was slapping, too. "But this surely won't be enough? I don't mean the Shoo, I mean the suggestion."

"I thought it might give him time to think. And give me time to think as well. It'll probably just make him mad at me, but even that might be helpful."

"If he did withdraw?" I asked, smearing midge repellent.

"I simply don't know. All we can do is wait and see."

We waited.

* * *

When at length we went back to Eilean na Roin we got a bit of a fright, which, I suppose, served us right. As the dusk had deepened, a merciful little wind had got up and begun to stir the bracken, but we fully expected to find a furious and agitated Mr. Bagshaw waiting at the causeway rubbing at his midge-bites and ready to agree to anything as long as he need never see the island again. But there was no sign of him, and when we called, there was no reply.

"They've driven him over the cliff and into the sea," said Crispin, but nobody laughed. To someone like Mr. Bagshaw, not used to the Highlands and, moreover, only just freed from a rather restricted form of life, the rocky island could hold, in the half-light, some very real dangers.

"I've been a double-dyed fool," said Neil, explosively. "Come on, let's find him. Crispin, you'd better stay put. Tie the boat up will you, please? Come on, Rose."

He led the way uphill at a fast pace, and I followed. We paused, but without much hope, at the tent.

"If he'd been in here, he'd have heard us," said Neil. "Are you there? Mr. Bagshaw?"

No reply. He pulled the flaps open to show an empty tent.

"I can hear the gulls at the cliff," I said, with misgiving.

"Only a few. Don't worry, nothing's happened, I'm sure. He struck me as having a lot of sense. I'll go over there, I know the ground better than you. You go the other way, downhill, towards the seal rocks, and take care. . . . Mr. Bagshaw! Are you there?" He strode away and was soon lost to sight in the growing dusk.

On the seaward side of the island the rising breeze was stronger, and waves boomed and echoed against the rocks. Some of the birds, disturbed, were out and calling. My eyes were used to the half-light, but even so the going was uneven, and needed care. I heard Neil call out a couple of times, but then the wind noises and the sea noises and the lie of the land blotted his voice out. I did not pause to listen for the enchanted sounds of the other island nights. I hurried, trying not to feel the older, stronger enchantment of the lonely Highland places, where the ghosts walk of all the dead, and the following shadows thicken your blood with cold.

I was almost at the seal rocks when I found him. I heard him first. Not the moan or cry for help that by now I was half expecting, but a soft, impatient shushing noise that came from a small figure kneeling, hunched, over something on the ground.

"Mr. Bagshaw! Oh, thank goodness! I was so afraid. . . . Are you all right?"

"Hush up, lass! Keep your voice down! Of course I'm all right, but there's a bird here with a broken wing or something, and you'll frighten it if you shout. . . . Careful now, slowly . . . Here, see."

I saw. Below him, barely visible in the deep shadow of a fallen-in rabbit's scrape, a small black bird lay, half hidden by dust and pieces of broken turf. One wing, curved and narrow, protruded from the debris, moving feebly. The small body quivered and shifted, as if its feet, under the weight of dust, were still trying for takeoff. But it was trapped. Behind it was the rabbit-hole, and to either side the turf bank rose sharply, where the recent fall of sandy stuff had half buried it, shutting it in like a golf ball in a bunker.

Mr. Bagshaw was making no attempt to

touch it. He backed off a pace. "If it's got a
wing broken—" he began.

I knelt down, and began very gently to
scrape away some of the fallen stuff. It was
sandy, light and friable, and moved easily.
"Look," I said, "the other wing's out now,
and it's moving it. Not damaged, then . . . I
don't think it's hurt at all. It must have just
been coming out of the burrow when that
bit of the bank came down and trapped it.
It looks recent."

"It is. I did it. I thought I heard something
funny from under ground, and then I
stepped too near the edge of the rabbit-
hole. Could have broken my ankle in the
dark."

"I know. I'm sorry. It was stupid of us,
really, to go off like that, but you see, we
were hoping . . ." I stopped. I could hardly
tell him what we had been hoping.

"Never mind," said Mr. Bagshaw. "But
how about getting this little bird out of here?
If we scrape the stuff away gently . . . yes,
that's fine. What's it doing in a rabbit hole
anyway? There, now, there, now . . . I'm
used to birds. I like them. We kept pigeons
when I was a boy, and my grandfather used
to breed canaries. That was in the days

when they bred them at the pithead to find the fire-damp. I used to help him. He kept them in the engine-shed, and you should have heard them all singing whenever the engine was running to lift the cage in the shaft. . . ," He was speaking almost in a whisper, while he gently shuffled the dust and fragments of turf aside, and I scattered them away. "I think you're right, the wings are OK. But—oh, here's your brother coming. He wants to watch himself in this light."

"What is it?" asked Crispin, limping up. Neil must have heard our voices, too. I saw him coming downhill towards us.

"A bird, here on the ground. A house martin, I think. It can't fly. I thought it might be hurt, but your sis says not."

"A house martin? Here?" And indeed, with the sickle wings spread, and the white rump now clearly visible in the dusk, Mr. Bagshaw's guess was fair enough.

"It's a stormy petrel," I said. "I've never seen one before, close to, but that's what it's got to be. And it's grounded. At least I hope that's all that's wrong."

My brother laid the crutch aside and knelt down. Neil joined us, with a question, and I said quickly: "It's OK. He's here. One of your petrels in trouble, that's all."

Crispin was saying quietly, to Mr. Bagshaw. "Rose is right. I don't think it's hurt. Why don't we just lift it out of there and give it a start?"

He reached down, but I caught at his arm. "Mr. Bagshaw's used to birds. Let him do it."

My brother glanced up. I saw him hesitate, then he moved back and got to his feet.

"Go on, then, Mr. Bagshaw. Your bird, I think?"

"Sure." I felt Crispin relax beside me as Mr. Bagshaw slid gentle palms under the petrel's breast, folding the wings in and cradling the little creature firmly and expertly. It made no attempt to struggle. It looked very small and fragile in his hands, like a tiny bat with velvet wings. I smelled again the sharp, chemical smell that pervaded the broch wall.

"Well, what do you know about that?" said Mr. Bagshaw admiringly. "The little bugger spat at me."

Crispin laughed. "If it got on your clothes, you may as well put them on the bonfire.

You'll never get the smell out. Now, if we just take it somewhere near the edge of the cliffs . . ." He led the way across the turf. At this end of the island the cliffs were lowish, with stacks jutting from the swell and wash of white water.

We stopped a few feet from the edge. "This will do," said Crispin. "Throw it over now, into the sea."

Mr. Bagshaw turned to stare at him, his face a pale blur in the dimness. I could see his mouth opening to protest.

"Go on," said my brother. "Quickly. That's where it was going. It's a storm petrel. Except when they're nesting, they live at sea. Really. They follow ships, and they can swim if they have to. That little thing can fly any-where—anywhere, as long as it's at sea. Go on, throw it."

"You're the boss, doctor," said Mr. Bag-shaw, and threw. The tiny bird made a curve up into the air, turned over, flapping a couple of times, like a moth caught in a draft, and then fell in a great sweeping dive to the sea. For a few moments we could see it, a scud-ding speck, black against the luminous white of the breakers, then it was gone,

beating strongly out towards the open Atlantic.

Mr. Bagshaw was looking down at his
hands, curved as if they still held the warm
shape of the bird. "Well, I never did. I
wouldn't have believed that if you'd told me.
A pigeon, yes, maybe, but that little spelk
of a thing . . . What did you say it was?"

"A stormy petrel. They call them Mother
Carey's chickens. The storm birds. Very
small, very strong, very tough. I told you,
they spend all their lives at sea, except when
they come ashore to nest."

"And they nest on this island?"

"Yes." It was Neil who replied, and I
added:

"That was what you heard, Mr. Bagshaw.
It must have a nest in that burrow, and what
you heard under the ground was the bird
crooning on its egg. They only have one.
They sing every night. Its mate may just
have come in from the sea to change over
on the nest. Usually they wait till it's darker
than this."

"You don't say?" He looked out for a few
moments towards the deepening darkness
to the west, filled with the sounds of the
sea. He spoke to Neil. "You didn't tell me."

"No. We try to keep quiet about them because they're so rare, and so vulnerable
when they do come in to land."

"I see. And you didn't tell me about the
seals, either. Did you know there were a lot
of seals at the end there, on the rocks?
Some of them with young ones, too."

"Yes. I knew. The island's called Eilean na
Roin, which means Seal Island. They've
been here since—well, since long before the
broch. Long before men came here in the
Iron Age."

"I see," said Mr. Bagshaw again. "Well, I
don't know that I can actually . . . That is—"
He did not finish what he had been going
to say, but asked instead: "Did you get your
boat fixed?"

"Yes, thank you. And I think we ought to
get back to it and I'll get everyone home
before the wind gets any stronger. Shall we
go? Can you see your way, sir?"

"Sure I can. You give a hand to the doctor
here. And don't call me sir, my name's Hartley, but I get Hart as a rule. Now look . . ."
This as we started back towards the boat.
"I don't know if there's anywhere back in
the village where I can ask you to come and

have supper with me, but if there is, I'd be glad if you'd all join me there."

"I doubt if there is," I said. "No hotel, of course, and I don't think you could take three extra to wherever you're staying, without giving notice. But why don't we all go to the cottage? I can manage. Let's all go back there, and I'll fix something."

"And I'll run you home afterwards in the boat," said Neil.

We had reached the causeway. Mr. Bagshaw stopped and turned back to face the three of us. "I won't say no. I'd like that very much. And here and now I'd like to say thank you for this day. I've enjoyed it all, and that island there has been a rare privilege, and something more than I expected."

There was a silence that could be felt. Then Neil stepped forward and put out a hand to help Mr. Bagshaw into the boat. "It's been rather more than any of us expected, I think," he said. "Can you see, Hart? Then let's go."

CHAPTER 21

It was a good supper. Since everyone in Moila knows everything, and Archie McLaren would certainly have broadcast yesterday's proceedings, and of course Mr. Bagshaw had seen no reason to make a secret of his plans, Mrs. McDougall had assumed that he might stay to supper at the big house, and be taken back to his lodgings by boat, so she had helped me out by sending down with Archie that morning a bag of freshly picked— presumably hydroponic—green beans, an apple pie of her own baking, and half a dozen rolls. Neil handed them over to me, and I made that most delicious of standbys, a macaroni cheese, which we ate with bacon and beans, with the apple pie to follow.

Mr. Bagshaw, remarking that this was the best food he had tasted in a very long time, ate with great enjoyment. The burning subject of the house sale was not even touched on. Neil, who still looked tired, said little, and the bulk of the conversation was between Mr. Bagshaw and Crispin. The former obviously regarded my brother as an expert on birds, and asked more questions about the petrels, and in his turn Crispin asked about the vanishing art of canary breeding. This led naturally to reminiscences of Mr. Bagshaw's childhood in some remote mining village near Durham, and so the meal passed pleasantly enough, and more easily than I had anticipated.

Neil helped me with the clearing and the coffee. As we waited for the kettle to boil he said, softly: "I can't thank you enough. I couldn't have coped on my own."

"That's all right. Did you gather from what he said that he's planning to leave tomorrow?"

"Yes. I did make a sort of offer of a bed, as I thought there would still be a lot to talk about, but he said he wanted to be back in the village to get the ferry in the morning. So your guess is as good as mine. But—" He stopped.

"But?"

He lifted his shoulders in a tired shrug. "But whatever comes in the near future, I do most passionately want to see this place left in peace. Aunt Emily used to call it her ivory tower." He gave a little half-laugh. "Something everyone should have. They're getting rare."

"And expensive."

"That's the trouble. Well, we'll try and pay the price, if he'll only let us. Here, let me take that tray."

"I can manage. Neil, Crispin brought some brandy. It's in that cupboard, and you know where the glasses are. How about that?"

"Wonderful."

I carried the tray through and handed cups of coffee round. "Only instant, I'm afraid. How do you like yours, Mr. Bagshaw?"

"Milk and sugar, please. Thanks."

"And thanks to Crispin, brandy," said Neil, coming across with the glasses.

"Just what the doctor ordered," said Mr. Bagshaw, and laughed heartily at his own joke. "Thank you. That's plenty. And now—" He took a sip, raised his glass to me, and said, across it: "I'm not going to make a

speech, folks, I wouldn't know how, but
there's something I've got to say. And the
first thing is, how much I've enjoyed this little trip, and getting to know you folks. I can't
say that yesterday was anything great, and
I'm sorry for what happened with Neil and
that little rat Ewen Mackay, but it wasn't any
doing of mine, and you've all been good
enough to treat it as such, and not hold
things against me that weren't all my fault
neither—either. So here's to you, and thank
you, all of you, and specially you, Miss Rose,
for this." A gesture took in the table.

"You're welcome," I said, smiling. "I
thought you said you wouldn't know how to
make a speech? That was a pretty nice
one."

"I haven't done yet." He was looking at
Neil now. "You all know what I came for, and
about my plans for opening the island up. I
like the place, and it could be done. Boy,
could it be done! Except for two things."

"Which are?" This from Neil.

"You don't want to sell," said Mr. Bagshaw flatly, "and don't think I didn't get all
the things you let drop about the weather
and the roof leaking and the light failing and
no one coming to do the plumbing when the

toilet seized up, excuse me, Miss Rose. . . .
No, Neil, let me finish. Whatever you've
been told about this option business, there's
no way I could make you sell if you didn't
want to, and after today, there's no way I
would make you, either. Because of the second thing."

This time no one spoke. He took a sip of
brandy.

"That island, the seal island, you called
it. There's a romantic little spot if there ever
was one, history, nature, good beach, nice
harbour, the lot. But it would take a rhinoc-
eros to want to sunbathe on those beaches,
and you can't tell me you didn't know it.
What the hell are they?"

"Midges," said Neil. "Argyll variety." He
set his glass down. The colour had begun
to come back into his face. He spoke so-
berly. "Mr. Bagshaw—Hart—I owe you an
apology. We all do. I feel ashamed about
today, and I've no right to be thanked for it.
It was a—well, it was a conspiracy to make
you hate the place. It was also stupid of us
to think you wouldn't see it. And to leave
you deliberately—yes, of course it was de-
liberate—on the island at the time when the
midges are worst. . . . That was childish, a

rotten thing to do. The only excuse is that you . . . you seemed so keen, and I honestly did think I would be held to it. And you took it all so well. You make me feel ashamed, and I beg your pardon. I hope you'll forgive me."

"And me," I said. "You've been sweet, Mr. Bagshaw, and I'm sorry."

"For what? Giving me my favourite supper? Forget it. You"—this to Neil—"are a very lucky man."

Neil looked blank. I felt myself go scarlet. Crispin smiled into his brandy glass.

Mr. Bagshaw pushed his chair back. "And now I'd better be going. Neil, you and I can talk on the way back in the boat. And don't feel bad about it. As far as I'm concerned, there's plenty of good fish in the sea still, and I'll find some place where I won't be doing Mother Whosit's chickens out of a roost, and where I can get the john mended the same day. I'll say good night, then, Miss Rose, and thanks again and no hard feelings. Crispin—"

My brother was on his feet. "I'll see you to the boat. Leave the dishes till I get back, Rose."

He went out with Mr. Bagshaw, the latter

waiting to help him carefully down the steps to the path. Neil smiled at me. The tired look had dropped away.

"I ought to make a speech, too. Thank you for today, and I really mean that. It's been quite a day, and I don't know where I'd have been without you. Shall I see you again soon?"

"I'll be here. The ivory tower is mine for another six days."

"For as long as you like, and rent-free at that," said my landlord. "Crispin's missed a whole week as it is, so why not stay over and make it up? I'll fix it for you with the agents. Now I really must go. I'm just hoping that the lawyers or the police won't drag me straight back to Glasgow, but I'll be round with the boat just as soon as I can make it. So—see you soon. And in any case—"

"Yes?"

"See you next term," he said, and went.

The sound of the boat's engine died. Crispin came back to help with the dishes, and then he went up to bed while I set the place tidy for the night. Before I locked the door I went outside, and down the steps to the edge of the beach. Crispin's light was out already. My own tiredness had gone, but I welcomed the silence and the solitude.

It closed me round, the blessed silence, made up of all the peaceful sounds of night; the whisper of sea on the shingle, the breeze in the bracken, the rustle of some creature in the grass, a splash from the tide's edge, and a movement among the rise and fall of the sea-tangle, dark in the dark.

"Good night," I whispered, and went indoors to bed.

I was just falling asleep when, from somewhere just outside the bay, I heard a boat's engine mutter softly past.

"See you next term," I said, and smiled into my pillow.

I believe I was still smiling when I fell asleep.